The Immigrant

A Hamilton County Album

Cover designed by Bill Toth
Book designed by Iris Bass

The Immigrant

A Hamilton County Album

Mark Harelik

AVAILABLE
PRESS

BALLANTINE BOOKS • NEW YORK

This play is dedicated
to
Haskell Harelik
1889–1987

This is his story and our story.

SEPTEMBER 1987

vi

It is a strange thing—to be an American . . .
Neither a place it is nor a blood name.
America is West and the wind blowing.
America is a great word and the snow.
A way, a white bird, the rain falling,
A shining thing in the mind and the gull's call . . .

This, this is our land, this is our people,
This that is neither a land nor a race . . .
A word's shape it is, a wind's sweep.
America is alone: many together,
Many of one mouth, of one breath,
Dressed as one—and none brothers among them:
Only the taught speech and the aped tongue.
America is alone and the gulls calling . . .

This is our land, this is our ancient ground—
The raw earth, the mixed bloods and the strangers,
The different eyes, the wind, and the heart's change.
These we will not leave though the old call us.
This is our country—our earth, our blood, our kind.
Here we will live our years till the earth blind us.

ARCHIBALD MACLEISH

DI GRINE KUSINE

Tsu mir iz gekummen ah kusine.
Shain vie gelt iz zie gevain di greene,
Baykelach vie roite pomerantzen,
Fiselach vos betten zich tsum tantsen.

Zie iz nit gegangen nor geshprungen.
Zie hot nit gerett nor gezungen.
Fraylich lustik iz gevain ihr meene.
Ot azay givehn iz mein kusine.

Herelach in goldene gelockte,
Tsaindelach vie perelech getockte,
Oigelach vie teibelach ah tsvilling,
Lipelach vie karshalach in frilling.

Ich hob zich bakent mit mein nextdorke,
Zie hot gehot a millinery storke.
A job hob ich gekrigen far di greene,
Az leben zol Columbus's medine.

Paide hot zie a lange tseit geklieben.
Fin mein kusine iz ah helft geblieben.
Die bekelach vie roite pomerantsen
Hoben zich shoin ois gegreent in gantsen.

A boy hot zie zich shoin ois gefinnen.
Er hot bei ihr die paide tsegenimmen.
Oif yeden shrit un trit flaig er zie vatchen.
Yede nacht flaig er zie gut ois patchen.

Es iz shoin fargangen ah pur yohren.
Fin mein kusine iz a tell gevoren.
Unter ihre bloye shaine oigen
Shvartse passen hoben zich getsoigen.

Yetst az ich begaigen mein kusine,
Fraig ich ihr vos machst du epes, greene.
Entfert zie mir mit ah troirige meene
Az brenen zol Columbus's medine.

DI GRINE KUSINE

(The Greenhorn Cousin)

Once a cousin came to me.
Pretty as gold was she, the greenhorn,
Cheeks like red oranges,
Tiny feet begging to dance.

She didn't walk, but skipped.
She didn't talk, but sang.
Her manner was gay and cheerful.
That's how my cousin used to be.

Hair in golden locks,
Little teeth like a string of pearls,
Little eyes like twin doves,
Little lips like spring cherries.

I introduced her to my neighbor,
The one with a millinery store.
I got a job for my cousin,
Long life to Columbus's land.

She worked for wages for many years
Until only half of her was left.
The cheeks like red oranges
Are now entirely green.

She had found herself a boy.
He took away all her money.
He watched every move she made.
Every night he beat her.

The years have now gone by.
My cousin has become a wreck.
Under her pretty blue eyes
Black lines are now drawn.

Now when I meet my cousin,
I ask how are you, greenhorn.
She says with a sorrowful face
To hell with Columbus's land.

WHERE SHALL I BE?

REFRAIN: *Where shall I be when the first trumpet sounds?*
Tell me, where shall I be when it sounds so loud?
When it sounds so loud as to wake up the dead,
Tell me, where whall I be when it sounds?

CHORUS: *When judgment day is drawing nigh,*
Where shall I be?
And God the works of men shall try, oh,
Where shall I be?
When east to west the fire shall roll,
Where shall I be?
How will it be with my poor soul, oh,
Where shall I be?

(REFRAIN.)

When wicked men his wrath shall see,
Where shall I be?
And to the hills and mountains flee, oh,
Where shall I be?
When rocks and mountains fall away,
Where shall I be?
And all the works of men decay, oh,
Where shall I be?

(REFRAIN.)

All trouble gone, all conflict passed,
Where shall I be?
And old Appolyon bound at last, oh,
Where shall I be?
When love shall reach from shore to shore,
Where shall I be?
And peace abide forever more, oh
Where shall I be?

(REFRAIN.)

CHARACTERS

HASKELL HARELIK (rhymes with garlic)
The immigrant. He arrives at the Port of Galveston
at the age of nineteen. A Russian Jew.

LEAH HARELIK
His wife. Three years younger than Haskell.

MILTON PERRY
Owner of the Perry National Bank of Hamilton,
Texas. A rock-solid, unyielding man. Forty to forty-
five years old.

IMA PERRY
His wife. Ten years his junior.

The scenes, aside from the Prologue, are various lo-
cales in and around Hamilton, a tiny agricultural com-
munity in central Texas, from 1909 to the present.

NOTE: The original production of this play was ac-
companied by projections of photographs and clip-
pings from the Harelik family album. As the pages of
the play turned, so did the pages of the album.

PROLOGUE

The slide projections and sounds introduce us into the countryside of Byelorussia, the heartland of the Russian-Jewish people. We hear a simple balalaika tune, "Di Grine Kusine." Pictures of Russian farmlands gradually become pictures of Jewish village life. Intruding into this pastoral scene come the sights and sounds of the pogrom: the mad clatter of invading hoofbeats, the shouts and cries. We see the IMMIGRANT standing in the center of the stage. The noises whirl around HIM. We hear whispers of "America, America," and

shortly the images are those of escape, of train travel, of masses of refugees crowding onto boats in German ports. A lengthy and difficult crossing of the Atlantic, packed into steerage. The arrival at the port of entry. Not Ellis Island, as we might expect, but the Port of Galveston, Texas, in the summer of 1909. The IMMI-GRANT is lost, hungry and bewildered. We hear cries of Texas longshoremen, Mexican longshoremen, and the general hubbub surrounding an active port. One of the centers of activity is the unloading of South Ameri-can banana boats. We hear Texan and Spanish voices hawking bananas.

The blast of a boat whistle blacks out the stage, and one immigrant's American life begins.

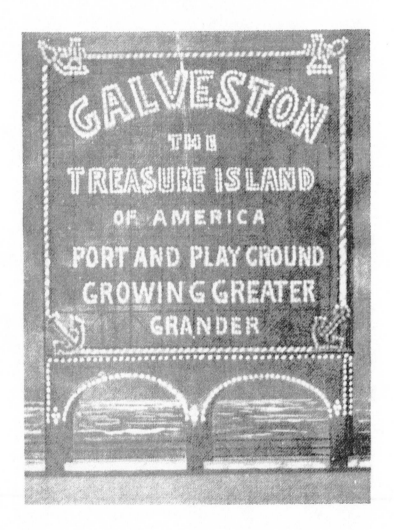

ACT ONE

Scene One

Hamilton, Texas, 1909. The clear, tuneful song of a mocking-bird brings up the lights on the front porch of MILTON and IMA PERRY, and the street. IMA is watering plants on the porch.

IMMIGRANT
(Offstage.)
    Pananasapennyapiece! Pananasapennyapiece!

(HE enters, hauling a ramshackle wheelbarrow filled with bananas, some fresh, some horribly rotten. HE is wearing the traditional long black coat, prayer-shawl vest, and short-brimmed cap of the Orthodox European Jew.)

    Pananasapennyapiece!

(IMA stares at HIM. After a moment, HE moves a few feet down the street, then is overcome by a sudden dizziness.)

IMA
(Calling through the screen door.)
    Milton! Milton! There's somebody out front!

MILTON
(Offstage.)
    Who is it?

IMA
    I don't know. He don't look good.

MILTON
(Offstage.)
    What?

3

IMA
>He looks sick, Milton. You better come look.

MILTON
(Offstage.)
>Stay where you are.

(HE joins HER on the porch.)

>Hey!

(From the barrow, the IMMIGRANT has pulled HIS water bottle, its lid dangling. When MILTON calls to HIM, HE gestures toward THEM with the empty container.)

IMMIGRANT
>Kennt ihr mir geb'n ah bissel vasser? (Can you give me a little water?)

MILTON
>Get inside. Get.

IMA
>Who is he?

MILTON
>Do what I say now.

IMMIGRANT
>Ich darf ah bisseleh vasser. Nur genook ontsufill'n mein flasch. (I need a little water. Only enough to fill my bottle.) Vasser.

MILTON
>Oh. Well, you can get some "wasser" at the well at the side of the house.

(The IMMIGRANT doesn't understand.)

At the *side* of the house. *There.* Wasser. Get going.

IMMIGRANT
(HE starts toward the well, then hopefully:)
Pananasapennyapiece!

MILTON
No bananas.

IMMIGRANT
Thank you.

(HE exits.)

MILTON
Best find some shade!

IMA
Milton, who was that?

MILTON
Banana pedlar. Wandering around, I expect. I give him some water.

IMA
Well, I'll swan. . . . He scared the daylights outta me.

MILTON
No harm long as he keeps moving, I expect.

5

THE IMMIGRANT

(HE goes inside leaving IMA on the porch.)

IMA
(With relief.)
  Well!

Scene Two

The town square, the next day. Holding a small pot of grease, the IMMIGRANT is greasing a frozen axle with HIS fingers. HE is quite dirty. IMA enters, shopping basket in hand.

IMA
   Well! Hello!

IMMIGRANT
   Hello.

IMA
   You were at our house yesterday. My husband gave you some water.

IMMIGRANT
   Enschuldig mir. Ich farshtay dir nit. Ich ken nit redd'n Aynglsh. (Excuse me. I don't understand you. I can't speak English.) No Aynglsh.

IMA
Oh. Well . . . of course.

(Speaks louder.)

My husband gave you some water! Yesterday!

(SHE makes a drinking gesture.)

Water!

IMMIGRANT
Vasser?

(HE holds up HIS water bottle.)

IMA
Yes.

(HE offers the bottle.)

No, thank you!

(HE returns to HIS work.)

I'd like some bananas, please.

IMMIGRANT
(Muttering.)
Oy! Yetst zeh vill'n koif'n pananas. Zeh vart'n biz
meine hent zeinen f'shmutsik mit fetz, un z'vill'n
koif'n tsvay toots! (Now they buy bananas! Wait
until my hands are covered with grease and order
two dozen!) Az me shmirt di reder, geyt der vog'n.
(As the wheels are greased, so the wagon rolls.)

8

(HE laughs at his quip. IMA is bewildered.)

Pananas. Yoh. Pananasapennyapiece.

(HE indicates that HIS hands are too filthy to handle the goods.)

Ich bin tsoo shmutsik. Shmuts, shmuts, shmutsik! Nehm vos d' darfst. (I'm too dirty. Dirt, dirt, dirty! Take what you need.) Uh . . . take.

IMA
Oh. Well . . . These look good. . . .

(SHE takes five and offers HIM a nickel. HE starts to take it and sees how filthy HIS hands are.)

IMMIGRANT
Ich bin tsoo schmutsik. (I'm too dirty.)

(HE opens the cigar box and gestures for HER to put the coin in.)

Ch'bayte. (Please.)

IMA
(Seeing how empty the box is.)
Well, I'll swan.

(Drops the nickel in, then points out a nearly blackened bunch.)

Those're getting awful ripe, you know. You really ought to sell those pretty quick.

(SHE takes them.)

I could make some good bread with these.

IMMIGRANT
(Taking them from HER.)
    No, no, no.

IMA
    Well, they're only gonna get worse on you.

IMMIGRANT
(With much pantomime.)
    Diyeh ess ich. (These, I eat.) Diyeh fa koif ich.
    (These I sell.) Pananasapennyapiece. No pananasa-
    pennyapiece. Nit goot.

IMA
    Oh Dora.

*(All composure having fled from HER charitable impulse,
SHE grabs some hefty bunches and fills HER basket to
overflowing. SHE then hurriedly empties HER coin purse
into the cigar box.)*

I'm sure that'll cover it.

*(SHE has given HIM too much money. HE grabs a quarter
and tries to return it to HER.)*

No. No. Much obliged. Never mind.

(SHE leaves, flustered.)

IMMIGRANT
(Calling after HER.)
  Much o . . . o . . . Okay.

(HE puts the quarter back in HIS cash box, then casts a sharp look in the direction in which SHE left. After a moment's consideration, HE removes HIS wedding ring, pockets it, and exits after HER with the wheelbarrow.)

Scene Three

The Perry front porch. MILTON seated with newspaper. Enter IMA with bananas.

IMA
Milton . . . I ran into that pedlar on the square. The one from yesterday?

(MILTON looks at the bananas, then looks at HER.)

Well, I know. I'll swan if I didn't start buying bananas like I was going into business for myself. I'll make some bread and take it around. You don't get enough fresh fruit besides . . .

MILTON
(Returning to HIS paper.)
Still in town, huh?

IMA
Yeah. You know, it don't seem practical to me, hauling them bananas in the sun like that.

MILTON
Well, they look fresh enough to me.

IMA
No, but I mean, Milton, it's not the bananas. It's him. He doesn't even have a horse. He's pulling this wheelbarrow around in this heat with his own back.

MILTON
Yes. Well . . .

IMA
Well . . . I tried to talk to him but he doesn't have
any English.

MILTON
No, German, I expect. Now, listen, Ima. I know
what's on your mind and I'm discouraging you right
now. This is not a charitable institution we're running here. Now if the banker's wife adopts every
itinerant pedlar that pulls his barrow through town,
then what does that say about the banker? Let well
enough alone. We run our business and he'll run his.

IMA
No, I know that. . . .

(SHE peels a banana for HIM.)

Here. Have one.

*(HE takes the fruit and SHE sees the IMMIGRANT
hesitating at the far edge of the yard.)*

IMMIGRANT
Hello.

IMA
Hello.

MILTON
Get in the house.

(SHE retreats but doesn't leave.)

13

IMMIGRANT
(In English.)
   Hello. Sir.

MILTON
   We've got plenty of bananas. Don't need any more
   bananas. They're good.

IMMIGRANT
   Um . . . yoh . . . um . . .

MILTON
   What can I do for you?

IMMIGRANT
   No pananas.

(HE fumbles inside the cart.)

   No pananasapennyapiece . . .

MILTON
(As IMA edges out.)
   Ima, did I tell you to get inside?

IMA
   Milton, look.

IMMIGRANT
*(He has taken a tightly rolled blanket from the cart. HE uses
it as a visual aid.)*
   Ich schloff shoin uff d'ayrd f' die letste tsvay voch'n.
   Hob g'shloff'n uff d'ayrd. Ich bin farmahtert. Ich

14

hob g'tracht . . . efsher kennt ihr mir farding'n ah tsimmer? Ich bin nit shtendik cha zoy shmutsik. Shmuts, shmuts, shmutsik! (I've been sleeping on the ground for the last two weeks. Sleeping on the ground. I'm tired of it. I was thinking . . . if you could rent me a room. I'm not usually so dirty. Dirt, dirt, dirty.)

IMA
I think maybe he wants to clean up. *Do you want to clean up?*

MILTON
No, that's not what he's after. What do you want?

IMMIGRANT
Ich vill ah tsimmer. Ah tsimmer. Ahn orret vie ts'shloffen. Ts'shloffen. (I want a room. A room. A place to sleep. To sleep.)

(HE gets on the ground.)

MILTON
Here now! Get up from there!

IMA
Milton, don't touch him! He might be sick!

MILTON
He's not sick.

(To the IMMIGRANT.)

I know what you want, and I'm afraid it's not possible. We're not a boarding house.

15

IMA
Well, Milton, maybe we ought to give him . . .

(MILTON turns on HER.)

I mean if he needs something . . .

MILTON
Ima, I'm proud to help a man who's in trouble. But there's hard times all over and he can clearly fend for himself.

(To IMMIGRANT.)

No. I'm sorry. No. If you want some water, the well is at the side of the house. Help yourself.

(MILTON turns to go and the IMMIGRANT looks to IMA. MILTON turns back.)

Help *yourself.*

(MILTON heads for the house.)

IMA
Milton . . .

MILTON
Let's go.

(IMA gives the IMMIGRANT a final look as MILTON herds HER into the house. Then . . .)

IMMIGRANT
Milton!

(THEY stop.)

Ch'bayte! Vart. Ch'bayte. Milton, gib ah kook. (Please. Look. Please. Milton, look here.)

(HE pulls a sock from its hiding place.)

Ich vill es nit fahr um*zist*. Kook. Kook. (I don't want it for free. Look. Look.)

(HE withdraws three tightly-rolled bills.)

Gelt! Ich vill dir batsoln ah forroyce. Ich vill dir batsoln. Ich vill zich ohpvasch'n. Ich vill zich rehzieren. Ihr vet mir gleichen. (Cash. I'll pay you first. I'll pay you. I'll wash. I'll shave. You'll like me.)

(HE offers the money.)

MILTON
Three dollars, huh? It's a poor businessman that offers all his liquid assets for a place to sleep.

(IMMIGRANT puts two bills behind HIS back.)

Whoops! The offer's dropping. I'd best sell while I can still get a good price. So one, huh?

(Holds up a finger.)

Only one?

IMMIGRANT
(Holds up one finger.)
Ayn. Yoh? (One. Yes?)

17

(MILTON makes an "I don't know . . ." sound. The IMMIGRANT makes the same sound referring to the house. MILTON looks at HIM sharply, but HIS amusement can be detected. IMA laughs, covering HER mouth.)

MILTON
For the night, huh?

IMA
No, Milton! Shame on you.

(To IMMIGRANT.)

No. Not a whole dollar. I mean . . .

MILTON
Oh, settle down, Ima. I'm not gonna charge him a dollar for one night.

IMA
Well, you're not even gonna joke about it. You can see he's having a hard time understanding as it is. Now behave like a Christian.

(MILTON takes a bite of banana. IMA, to IMMIGRANT.)

We'd be proud to put you up.

(Points to the house.)

Yes!

(Putting HER cheek to HER hands, indicating sleeping.)

19

Yes!

IMMIGRANT
(to IMA.)
  Yoh?

(To MILTON.)

  Yoh?

(MILTON shrugs HIS shoulders, deferring to IMA. IMMI-GRANT is overcome for a moment.)
  Thank you. Thank you! Welcome! Voo zoll ich avek
  shtel'n mah vaygell? Voo zoll ich avek shtel'n diyeh
  zach? Diyeh idyottishe, ts'brochenneh, f'kockteh . . .
  (Where shall I put my cart? Where shall I put this
  thing? This idiotic, broken-down, shitty . . .)

MILTON
  Oh! You can put it over by the well.

(Pointing.)

  The well!

IMMIGRANT
(Remembering the word.)
  Well!

MILTON
  And while you're over there, wash up. Wasser.

IMMIGRANT
  Vasser, yah!

20

IMA
 I'll fetch soap and a towel.

(SHE goes.)

IMMIGRANT
 Nu. Ayn, yoh? (So. One, yes?)

(HE proffers the dollar bill.)

MILTON
 No.

IMMIGRANT
(Puzzled.)
 No . . . ?

MILTON
 Ten cents.

IMMIGRANT
 Ten?!

MILTON
 . . . cents.

IMMIGRANT
 Cents? Okay. Ten cents.

(HE fetches HIS cigar box and counts out ten pennies one by one.)

MILTON
 What's your name?

THE IMMIGRANT

IMMIGRANT
Ah! Meine papieren! (My papers!)

(HE pulls a customs certificate out of a sock.)

My name. My papers. Chatzkell Garehlik. Oif Aynglsh!

MILTON
Well, I'm Milton Perry. And this is my wife, Ima.

(SHE has returned with a sparkling white towel and a gigantic cake of soap.)

IMA
Here you go. Now you scrub up good.

HASKELL
Thank you. Thank you.

(HE starts out. Then, to IMA.)

Shmuts, shmuts, shmutsik!

IMA
Yeah!

(IMMIGRANT exits.)

That's good, Milton. Thank you.

MILTON
(Pours the pennies into HER hand.)
Here. Put that in the bank.

IMA
  Dora.

MILTON
  Chazkell.

IMA
  What?

MILTON
  It's his name. Chazkell Garlik. He's not German.
  He's Russian.

IMA
  Russian?! Well, I'll swan.

MILTON
  Russian. And a Jew.

IMA
(Silence.)
  Good heavens, Milton. I wonder if we haven't made
  a mistake. I mean, I didn't know he was a Jew. I just
  thought he was down on his luck.

MILTON
  Well, Jew or no Jew, he's paid ten American cents
  for a bed to sleep in and a deal's a deal. He seems all
  right. You just keep your distance.

IMA
  Where should we put him?

23

MILTON
He'll go upstairs.

IMA
That's Charlie's old room!

MILTON
It's an empty room. We might as well get some good out of it.

(IMA protests.)

Now behave like a Christian.

HASKELL
(Returns with clean face and hands. HE carries the soap and towel. Also HIS cash box and a book.)

Ah! Goot. Goot.

(HE returns the soap and towel.)

Thank you.

MILTON
(Returning HIS papers.)
Mm hmm.

(MILTON returns to HIS newspaper. HASKELL and IMA stand awkwardly.)

IMA
All right, then. The room is right upstairs, Mr. uh . . .

MILTON
  Garlik.

IMA
  Mr. Garlik.

(SHE goes into the house.)

HASKELL
(To MILTON, showing the certificate.)
  Gare*h*lik.

(Then, running after IMA.)

  Gare*h*lik. Chatzkell.

IMA
  Hezkell.

HASKELL
  No, no . . .

(HE demonstrates the guttural "ch" sound.)

  Chatzkell.

IMA
  H . . . hezkell.

HASKELL
  Yoh! Goot! Cha zoy vie ah yiddishe baleboosta!
  (Like a real Jewish lady!) Ah, Aynglsh!

(HE displays the book and reads the title.)

"Aynglsh Is Easy." Az ah *yohr* off im, "Aynglsh Is Easy"! (He should *have* such a year!)

IMA
This was my . . .

(SHE gestures around.)

This is for you.

HASKELL
(Amazed.)
Thank you.

(SHE starts to leave, but HE stops HER and looks up a page in HIS primer.)

Good. Night. Ima.

IMA
Good night.

(SHE thinks for a moment.)

Haskell.

HASKELL
Yoh! Goot!

(SHE leaves and HASKELL runs to the door, calling out.)

HASKELL
Milton! Thank you!

MILTON
(IMA comes onto the porch, fretting.)
Well, set down and relax, you might as well. You wanted him in, he's in.

IMA
  Well. I don't mind him much.

MILTON
(Sardonically.)
  Yeah, I expect I couldn't resist him, either.

IMA
  He's a long way from home.

MILTON
  Long ways, yes.

(In HIS room, HASKELL is practicing from HIS primer, first reading, then repeating.)

HASKELL
  Good morning. It is a beautiful day. Good morning.
  It is a beautiful day.

(Together.)

IMA
  What do you expect
  he's doing here?

HASKELL
  How are you?

HASKELL
  How are you?

MILTON
  Starting from scratch, sounds like.

HASKELL
  I am a stranger here. I am a stranger here.

27

Scene Four

The Perry front porch. IMA seated, MILTON working in the yard. HASKELL enters from the well, exhausted. HE carries his cigar cash box and one blackened banana.

MILTON
  Good evening, Haskell.

HASKELL
  Hello, Milton.

IMA
  Haskell.

HASKELL
  Ima.

(HE passes THEM on the porch and shuffles into the house.)

MILTON
  He give me *rent* money this morning.

IMA
  Did he now?

MILTON
  Come down to the bank and stood outside till some-body called me. Two weeks *rent* money. For *his* room, he says.

IMA
  Just from them bananas. I'll swan if that boy ain't a

natural salesman, then I don't know what. Miz Genther carried me over two dozen of banana muffins this morning. I traded her a loaf of banana bread. If he don't switch to something else, before long this town's gonna swing in the trees.

(HASKELL enters HIS room.)

MILTON
I didn't know what to do. He just give it to me.

IMA
That boy's savin' hard. He's savin' hard and it ain't just for himself, you mark my words. He's got somebody. . . . family or something.

(The focus of the scene shifts to HASKELL's room. He is writing a letter with a picture before HIM.)

HASKELL
Meine fishele Leah, Nochamahl shalom f'n d' United States f'n Amerikeh. Un' shalom f'n Hamilton, Texas. Ah toizent tsvay hundert mensch'n . . .

(As HASKELL speaks, HIS recorded voice takes over in English.)

My sweet Leah, hello again from the United States of America. And hello from Hamilton, Texas, population one thousand and two hundred. Do you remember looking at the maps and wondering what this Texas was? Well, I'll tell you, we had no idea. After the stories we heard of New York, I got off this boat and fell forward into a great open plain.

Tiny little towns. But one of these tiny places appeals to me very much. Hamilton, it's called. Population one thousand and two hundred. They have a sign before you enter the town that tells you this very clearly. How long would I have to stay, I wonder, before someone is required to change that number?

The banana business is very good. The produce train comes to a town nearby, only a two-day walk. And the bananas I buy—two, three stalks at a time—have immigrated through the same port at Galveston. We're both strangers here, these bananas and I, but such country we've come to! Such wealth! Do you know that this little town has not one but two banks? And do you know something else? I'm living in the house of a banker! Yes! I've been in my own room, sleeping on a bed with springs for a week now. His name is Milton Perry, his wife, Ima. Strange names, aren't they? Also strange to be in a land with no shul, no rabbi, no Jews at all. Some days I'm as lonely as a stone. But at other times, most times, I simply feel free. I sprawl on the ground and look at the stars as they look at you. Tiny mirrors that, I used to think, reflect the splendor of unreachable lands. Now they reflect tomorrow's sun—the daylight that will fall on the shoulders of your Haskell. At last, Leah, something is happening. Something is happening! God bless you and keep you, my darling Leah, until I can stand by your side again.

(Then live.)

Die tseit vet avek flee-ehn meine fishele! (The time will fly, my sweet.)

(The focus shifts back to the PERRYs.)

IMA
What in the world?

HASKELL
(Recorded voice.)
  It won't be long.

MILTON
  That was him.

HASKELL
(Recorded voice.)
  Haskell.

IMA
  Well, Dora, you think he's having a nightmare? I
  don't know, Milton. He's killing himself the way
  he's scraping those pennies together.

MILTON
  Well, it's in the blood, don't you imagine? A Jew is
  tight with a dollar, they say.

IMA
  Do they now? Shame on you, Milton.

*(SHE goes into the house and stops before HASKELL's
door. HASKELL is placing bills into the envelope. SHE
knocks.)*

  Haskell? Haskell?

HASKELL
  Yoh! Yoh! Uh, vart ah moment, ch'bayte. (Yes.
  Yes. Uh, wait a moment, please.)

*(HE hides the letter and photo behind HIS back and flips
open the primer.)*

IMA
  Haskell?

HASKELL
  Yes? Hello?

IMA
(Entering.)
  Hello. I just . . . uh . . . You're all right now? You
  look awful tired.

(HE gestures weakly around the room.)

  Well . . . All right then . . . Good night, now.

HASKELL
(In English.)
  Good night.

(SHE starts to go.)

  Thank you.

IMA
  Oh. Well, you're welcome.

HASKELL
  Much . . . obliged.

IMA
  Well! Yes, indeed!

(SHE exits.)

Scene Five

MR. PERRY's office in the Perry National Bank Building.
MILTON is seated at HIS desk, smoking.

HASKELL
  Mr. Perry?

MILTON
  Yes? Oh! Come in, Haskell. Have a seat. Take off
  your coat.

  (HASKELL does so reluctantly.)

  Uh, you . . . you wanna . . . ?

  (HE indicates HASKELL's cap.)

HASKELL
  No! No, no.

MILTON
  OK. Well, how do you like our little town?

HASKELL
  Oh, good. Very good. I like . . .

(In very halting English.)

  . . . this place.

MILTON
  Not quite the same as it is in Russia, is it?

HASKELL
No. Hot. And . . . safe.

MILTON
Safe? Well now, I never thought of that. No, there's
not much trouble around here.

HASKELL
No.

MILTON
Sit down, Haskell. I'll be right with you.

(HE finishes up a signature.)

All right now, Haskell. I'm sorry to pull you away
from your, uh, banana cart and all, but I felt it was
necessary that we talk a little bit. Now, Haskell,
you've been our guest, so to speak, for nigh onto a
month now. . . .

HASKELL
Six . . .

MILTON
What?

HASKELL
Six weeks. On Tuesday. Six weeks.

MILTON
Is that a fact? So. I have to say that I haven't been
aware of much progress on your part.

HASKELL
    I . . .

MILTON
    Now just let me tell you what I'm talking about. I
    can see that you work hard with this . . . this banana
    business of yours. My wife has opened her house to
    you and I'm not saying you're not welcome. But
    your stay in our home was never meant to be a
    permanent situation and I hope that's not your
    impression.

(Pause.)

    Haskell, I feel that the way you're conducting your
    business is impractical.

HASKELL
(Doesn't understand the word.)
    Im . . . imp . . .

MILTON
    It's impractical. Now, you want a home of your
    own, don't you? A home? A house? Where you live?
    A house? You want your own . . .

HASKELL
(Not following.)
    A house. Yes. It's fine . . .

MILTON
    Good.

HASKELL
(Gesturing to MILTON's desk.)
  It's good!

MILTON
  Fine! Well . . . The point is I watch you bust your
  butt hauling a load of rotten bananas around . . .

HASKELL
  Bust . . . bust . . .

MILTON
  Bust your butt . . .

HASKELL
  Butt.

MILTON
  Yeah, your butt. Your ass. This thing.
(Gestures.)

HASKELL
(Gets up to look.)
  Yes?

MILTON
  No, no. Haskell, would you just sit down?

HASKELL
  I don't know.

MILTON
  I know you don't. Just sit.

(HASKELL does, and realizes what a butt *is.)*

Look, Haskell—your business . . . business?

HASKELL
Business, yes.

MILTON
. . . is not practical.

HASKELL
Not . . . ?

MILTON
It's not *efficient!* Your bananas go bad too soon. That
thing weighs a ton. You're breaking your back. You
have to sell too high a volume to turn a profit. Not
good! Now I want to ask you something, Haskell.
Do you intend to stay here? Stay in Hamilton?

HASKELL
Stay?

(Near tears.)

Yes, I stay.

MILTON
Are you prepared to take some advice? Because I
can't approve of the way you're going about this.

HASKELL
Tell me.

MILTON
All right, then, look. Get rid of those bananas. It's my feeling that a lot of your trade in the county has come from people just trying to help you out. And that won't support a business. It's bound to give out. But what people do need is what we call notions and sundries.

(HASKELL doesn't understand.)

Pots, pans, brooms, and things!

HASKELL
Yoh!

MILTON
There isn't a housewife in the county that doesn't need something like that every . . .

HASKELL
Mr. Perry. Listen. This kind business I know.

MILTON
Good! Now there's a fellow in Waco . . .

HASKELL
In Russia, mens do this. Sell for house. To the lady. Sometime cart. Sometime not cart. Carry. This mens we see him. This town, this town, this town. No house. No place. We call him luftmensch. Man of air. Dirty. Lost. In Russia, he is sad man. I say— never. Never like this. I come to America. To this Texas. And I do same. The cart. The walk. Carry. But no pots. No little string. No medicine. Fruit!

MILTON
Wait a minute, Haskell.

HASKELL
In Russia, nothing like this pananas! Yes cart. Yes walk. Yes dirty. But fruit! Sweet . . .

MILTON
Haskell, you're not listening. . . .

HASKELL
Mr. Perry—more fruit! Put more fruit!

MILTON
More fruit!

HASKELL
Yoh!

MILTON
Goddamn it, Haskell, I'm trying to talk you out of the bananas . . .

HASKELL
No, no! Different! Different kind! Many different kind!

MILTON
Now wait a minute.

HASKELL
Put the . . .

MILTON
Wait just a blue-eyed minute. You know you may

be right? Why not turn that barrow into a goddamn
fruit store? You could cut back on the bananas . . .

HASKELL
But the pananas . . .

MILTON
I didn't say chuck 'em. I just said cut back.

HASKELL
Cut back.

MILTON
And then work in some apples and oranges and
peaches, maybe. And grapefruit! You ever hear of
grapefruit?

HASKELL
Grape? Sure, for wine.

MILTON
No, no, no! I mean grape*fruit*! Big! Big yellow things!
Grow on trees!

HASKELL
Big yellow things?

MILTON
Yes! In the Valley, they have orchards and orchards
of 'em. All right, Haskell, you want fruit? Then
goddamn make it fruit!

HASKELL
Yes, it's good.

MILTON
  Good? Son, it's great. It's perfect. Now you're still
  going to have a heavy load, but a horse'll take care
  of that. Less spoilage and your diversity'll turn a
  greater profit. Now that's the American way. . . .

HASKELL
  Yoh. Not just American. Good . . .

MILTON
  Good sense.

HASKELL
  Sense.

MILTON
  Well, that's just what I'm talking about. Now there's
  a shipper in Galveston we can contract with. And
  your conveyance will need some modification.

HASKELL
  What does it mean, this . . . ?

MILTON
  Changes! Changes, Haskell! Some rows of shelves,
  and . . .

(Grabs paper and pencil.)

Look—a wagon. All right?

HASKELL
  Yoh?

MILTON
  Shelves. Two sets. On both sides. And room in the
  front and back for baskets and what-not. And a little
  roof on it, like this. And on top, a sign maybe.

HASKELL
  Yeah! Put the, uh . . . the, uh . . .

MILTON
  Your name.

HASKELL
  *Gareh*lik!

MILTON
  GARLIK'S FRUIT AND VEG . . . GARLIC'S FRUIT. No,
  that'll never work. *Har*lik. HARLIK'S FRUITS AND
  VEGETABLES. How's that sound?

HASKELL
  Eh . . .

MILTON
  And a horse. A horse to pull it.

HASKELL
  That's good! You draw very good!

MILTON
  Haskell, you're right. If you're going to be a businessman, then by God *be* a businessman, not a man-
  ual laborer. Now does that interest you?

HASKELL
  Yes.

MILTON
   Good sense?

HASKELL
   Yes!

MILTON
   Damn right. You're smart, Haskell. You work hard.
   I don't want to see you break yourself down.

HASKELL
   Yes. It's a good idea.

MILTON
   You bet it is.

HASKELL
   But no.

MILTON
   No?

HASKELL
   Idea is free. Two shelf, one horse not free. Cost
   money I don't . . .

MILTON
   I know that. I'm going to loan you the money. The
   horse and wagon'll be mortgaged to the bank and
   you'll pay me back. A little bit at a time. Now what
   do you think?

HASKELL
   What do I think? I think yes.

MILTON
  You shoot straight with me and I'll help you. You
  don't and you're out on your butt. Do you understand that?

HASKELL
  Butt, yes.

MILTON
  Good. Good boy. Now I'll draw up a proper contract, we'll sign it in the morning and get started.

HASKELL
  Good business, Mr. Perry. I give back.

MILTON
  Not another word, Haskell. We're . . . *partners* now.

(HE offers HIS hand. HASKELL, amazed, takes it.)

HASKELL
  Partners.

(HASKELL gathers the drawing).

MILTON
  And a partnership is built on trust. You don't jew
  me and I don't jew . . .

HASKELL
  It's good!

MILTON
  Sorry.

HASKELL
Sorry?

MILTON
Nothing. I'll see you at home.

HASKELL
At home, yes. You draw very good!

(HE exits.)

Scene Six

The lights come up on IMA on HER front porch, as MIL-TON enters the yard.

IMA
  Would you hurry up, mister? We're gonna be late for church.

MILTON
  Ima, you know I'm not going.

IMA
  Now why not, Milton? I thought this week you'd come with me.

MILTON
  Now why would I say anything like that?

IMA
  I wish you'd come.

MILTON
  Ima, I didn't go with you last week. I'm not going with you next week. It'd be plumb silly for me to go with you this week.

IMA
  You go ahead and make light, mister. You're gonna be awful sorry when your day comes.

MILTON
(As HE disappears into the house.)
  I'm sorry already.

(IMA exits.)

(As the following letter begins, HASKELL brings HIS new cart into the yard. A sign atop the cart's roof says HARELIK'S FRUITS AND VEGETABLES. *The produce is neatly arranged along shelves and in baskets. It is the end of the day and HASKELL throws a tarp over it before going inside for the night.)*

HASKELL
(Voice recorded.)
My precious Leah, I love to write to you. I hate to write to you. These months see only paper and ink passing between us and between times I pretend that I am with you, talking. I hear your reply. I answer. "It's dark now, Haskell. Time to come home, yes?" "Yes, you're right. I'm on my way." "And shouldn't you dress more warmly?" "You're sitting in Russia. Don't tell me how to dress in Texas." "My, Haskell! You're so stern!" And then my sternness falls to pieces and we kiss. But the kiss falls on paper and ink. And I hate these letters. . . .

(HASKELL goes into the house.)

Since I last wrote to you, we've moved into the new establishment. We've installed several rows of shelves. Oh yes, and we've added vegetables now and a new roof. And to the staff, we've added one horse. Very docile. No back talk.

(HASKELL enters HIS room, dons HIS skullcap and prayer shawl and begins HIS evening prayers.)

I assume you've opened the other envelope. Yes, it's true. Sit down. Stop crying. Part of the money will buy train passage from Minsk to Bremen. If they give you trouble at the border, you will have to sneak across, I'm afraid. Be prepared for that. The ticket is for steerage passage from Bremen to Galveston. You'll like steerage. Very pleasant. If you're lucky, they won't lock you in. If you're luckier still, you'll get a top bunk. Be strong, Leah. Forget politeness. Forget respect. Forget sleep. And for God's sake, don't carry more than you can hold at one time. Travel light, Leah. Travel as light as you can. Once in Galveston, the Texas Flyer train will take you to Gatesville where I'll be waiting.

Oh, hurry, Leahle, hurry. It's getting harder and harder for me to concentrate on these letters. Or on anything else these days. During my prayers, even, I drift away and daydream.

(A mockingbird sings outside the window. HE searches for it.)

Listen! Do you hear?

(It sings again.)

A bird with the most beautiful song in the world met me at my boat, led my every step to Hamilton, and currently resides outside my window. A mockingbird, it's called, and it sings with such piercing sweetness that I think my heart will break.

(It sings again. HASKELL breaks off in the midst of HIS prayers and stands at the window.)

That bird calls to me as I call to you. "Leave the past. Leave it. Travel light. Kiss your Mama goodbye and don't look back."

(HE removes HIS prayer shawl.)

I've awakened into my dreams, my love, and I can hear you beyond the horizon starting your long walk toward me.

(HE removes HIS skullcap and stands at the window.)

God bless you and keep you and take a deep breath! The next time you hear from me will be in person! Haskell.

Scene Seven

Before dawn. HASKELL enters from the house. HE removes the tarp from HIS produce wagon, then proceeds to remove the sign atop it. It is punctured by a large jagged hole. HE still wears HIS short-brimmed cap, but the prayer-shawl vest is gone.

IMA
(From within the house.)
   Haskell, are you still here?

HASKELL
   Yes, I'm just . . . still loading up.

(HE hastily puts the sign on the ground and partially covers it with the tarp.)

IMA
(At doorway.)
   Oh, good. Haskell, I need six more of them green apples. I'm gonna make another pie. I've got dough left over and we might as well keep one for ourselves.

HASKELL
   Yes, ma'am. Six green apples.

(SHE leaves the pie she has been holding on the porch and comes into the yard. She holds out HER apron, making a basket.)

   That's five cents.

THE IMMIGRANT

IMA
  Five? Are you sure?

HASKELL
  First customer of the day gets special price.

IMA
  Now I don't want you giving away any of your . . .

HASKELL
  No, no. It's good business.

IMA
  'Cause you need to save every nickel.

HASKELL
  I save nickels. Pennies, too.

IMA
  You must be sending to your folks.

HASKELL
  Mm hmm.

IMA
  In your letters.

HASKELL
  Yes.

IMA
  Good. Well, all right then, here you go.

(SHE pays.)

Oh, Haskell, I have an apple pie that needs delivering and I'd be much obliged if you could carry it for me.

HASKELL
Yes. That's fine.

IMA
Oh, good.

(SHE goes onto the porch to get it.)

I'm sending this out to poor old Miz Haggerty. She busted her hip chasing a hen across their pasture. Slipped in a wet cowflop—practically snapped in two.

(HE takes the pie.)

I'd have to laugh if it hadn't hurt her so bad. Now she's out in Lime Rock, you know.

HASKELL
Oh, Miz Perry, I can't take this pie.

IMA
Oh, Haskell, we could find room somewhere, I'm sure.

HASKELL
Please. I can't take it. I'm not going out to Lime Rock today.

IMA
Well, I don't understand. You've been going out
there every day.

(SHE sees the damaged sign on the ground.)

What in the world . . . ?

HASKELL
My customers on that road, they change their mind.

IMA
Is this a bullet hole? Haskell, what in the world
happened to you? Isn't this a bullet hole?

HASKELL
Yes.

IMA
Good Lord in heaven, boy, did somebody take a shot
at you?

HASKELL
No! Not at me. It was just, just to scare me, or . . .

IMA
The Peterson boys.

HASKELL
I don't know! I was on the road to Lime Rock. It's a
long stretch, you know. And it was green and cool,
and the birds and the horse sound like Russia. And I
daydream.

54

(A distant, ghostlike balalaika is heard.)

I thought I was there. And then I hear other horses
and the hoofbeats are very fast and I get scared
because this, too, is a memory I have. And then all of
a sudden here are five, six men and they stop me and
shake the cart and say . . . things. People I trade
with. I know them, but . . . something, they . . .
show me their guns and shoot this hole in the sign
and I run like hell. So. They scare me, I run. Maybe
it's just fun, but I don't think I go back to Lime
Rock today.

IMA
Haskell, you tell me who those men were and we're
going to do something about it right now. I just
can't believe that Christians would behave like that.

HASKELL
No, no.

IMA
Yes! We'll put a stop to it.

HASKELL
No, I just don't go back there.

IMA
Nonsense, Haskell. It's the Peterson boys, I'm sure
of it.

HASKELL
Miz Perry, please! Forget this. If we make trouble, it

will get worse. I promise you, I know this. Please. It
would anger them and you . . .

IMA
Well, I'm ashamed, Haskell. We're just not used to
. . . strangers. Some don't handle it like Christians.
It frightens the daylights out of me.

HASKELL
Yeah, scares me, too. I'm not a brave man. Even a
tiny thing, I cut my finger, it bleeds, it makes me
sick. I get scared, I run. I don't go back. It's not the
first time.

IMA
You amaze me, son. You leave your home, travel
thousands of miles, put on a new language, eat my
cooking. If that's not courage.

HASKELL
It's *not* courage. I just do it. And your cooking is
very good.

IMA
Well, you better say so! All right, you better hitch
up and run along. You're losing daylight.

(Something catches HER eye.)

What're you selling here, hornet's nests?

HASKELL
Hornet? Oh! Oh, no hornet nest. This is a brand
new vegetable.

IMA
Well, I'll swan. I didn't know there could be such a
thing.

HASKELL
Oh yes! Brand new. Hard-to-choke.

IMA
Say again?

HASKELL
(Holding up an artichoke.)
It's called hard-to-choke.

IMA
And you eat 'em?

HASKELL
Yes!

IMA
How?

HASKELL
I don't know! But it's new! I was too curious, so I
buy them and everyone says, "My Lord! What is
this?" And I say, "Hard-to-choke", and no one can
believe it!

IMA
Well, I *don't* believe it. Easy-to-choke, more likely.

HASKELL
Here. You take it.

(HE gives it to HER.)

If you can figure how to cook it, no charge.

IMA
Well . . . I'll give it a try. You're back early tonight?

HASKELL
Oh yes, Shabbos.

IMA
And that means Sabbath, don't it?

HASKELL
Yes! Very good! Shabbos, Sabbath.

IMA
Shabbos. It's such a pretty word. They sound so much alike, there's hardly any difference between the two.

HASKELL
(With a glance toward Lime Rock.)
Almost. So if the horse is still on his feet and I don't work him too hard, maybe we can get home in time.

(HE exits.)

IMA
Yes, all right.

(Looking after HIM; worried, wondering.)

Goodbye, then.

Scene Eight

The new shop on the square, a regular storefront building, housing HARELIK'S FRUITS AND VEGETABLES. MILTON is dragging and arranging one-hundred-pound bags of flour, rice, and potatoes into some semblance of order. HE is beat and irritable. IMA enters from the street.

IMA
   Well, they told me you were over here hauling beans. I had to come see for myself. My!

(The place looks pretty bleak.)

   The place looks nice. . . . Get these shelves filled up some, it'd be right proud. Is this all there is?

MILTON
   There's another load coming over this afternoon.

IMA
   Oh, good. Where's Haskell?

MILTON
   Driving the load.

IMA
   Oh, good. Milton, I wish you'd be careful. This suit's gonna be a mess.

(SHE tries to dust HIM off.)

MILTON
   Ima.

IMA
> Well, why're you doing all this by yourself, any-
> how? I thought Haskell took on a boy to help out.

MILTON
> He took on a boy, Ima. He's in the back doing the
> same thing I'm trying to do. Do you expect a ten-
> year-old child to do it all by himself?

(HE goes into the back room.)

IMA
(To HERSELF.)
> Bite my head off, why don't you?

MILTON
(A crash is heard.)
> Goddamn it!

IMA
> Please don't cuss. It's good of you to help out,
> anyway.

MILTON
(Re-entering.)
> Yeah. Helping out like a mule helps a plow.

IMA
> A good work is its own reward, Milton.

MILTON
(Glares at HER.)
> Don't you preach at me, woman. I'm here, aren't I?
> Playing poppa all over again? It's just not exactly

what I had in mind. Now are you prepared to accept that?

(HE rests.)

IMA
Well, it looks real nice. I'm glad to see him get permanent. Now at least he don't have to go *looking* for trouble. If folks want to trade, they can come to him.

MILTON
That's the question, isn't it?

IMA
Mm.

(SHE gazes out the door.)

You know, I've never looked so close at this town till he come. Kinda sets off the difference, I guess. I was afraid of him, was you? First time I heard him bucking out them evening prayers of his, I thought he'd raise the devil, for sure.

MILTON
Well, didn't he?

IMA
How do you mean?

MILTON
Them Peterson boys and the like.

IMA
Oh, come now, Milton. Those boys are purely mean.

MILTON
Yes, but he sure brought it out of them easy enough.

IMA
Milton!

MILTON
Well, goddamn it, there's a truth to that! I'm standing in front of the whole town to set up a Jew in
business—I don't know if anybody'll put one *foot* in
this place. The families in this county have been here
a long time. And we're not used to a foreigner—
Mexican, Niggra, any kind.

IMA
It's un-Christian, Milton.

MILTON
Yes! So's he!

IMA
Shame on you. That's not what I meant.

MILTON
Well, people change hard, is all I'm saying. And this
stuff rots.

*(HASKELL has entered during this last exchange. HE is
wearing work clothes and a straw work hat. When HE doffs
it after entering, he is bareheaded. HE will remain bareheaded for the rest of the play.)*

IMA
Haskell! Scare me to death.

MILTON
Well, let's get the load in.

HASKELL
No, stay. Stay just a minute. I need to consult with you. And you too, Ima. Please.

(Gesturing to THEM both.)

Sit. I think the business is growing very well. Who would think? We start from a stinking little wheelbarrow and now, thanks to both of you, here is this store full of goods, with a mortgage—a real American business. Soon, God willing, I move to my own house, but unfortunately not yet, so much money has to go here and . . .

MILTON
Haskell, I told you not to worry about that and I meant it.

HASKELL
Yes, well, thank you. So . . .

MILTON
So?

HASKELL
. . . so, I feel that with one employee—a good one—a good boy, yes?

MILTON
Yes.

HASKELLL
. . . that with one employee, the work is easier, is more efficient and . . . and . . . and . . . practical . . .

MILTON
Haskell, for Christ's sake, what is it?

HASKELL
So we need another employee.

MILTON
I'm getting back to the bank.

HASKELL
Milton, I think it's a good idea.

MILTON
Haskell, it's a very bad idea. It would be stupid to put on more help. You've been open for one day and . . .

HASKELL
I've been open for eleven months! I work hard. . . .

MILTON
This is ridiculous. I'm not gonna hear any more of this.

(HE starts for the door.)

HASKELL
Milton, please! My new employee . . .

MILTON
Your new employ . . . I don't believe this.

HASKELL
. . . is my wife!

(THEY are stunned.)

From Russia.

IMA
I knew it!

MILTON
You've been deceiving us, boy.

HASKELL
No, no. Every day I was going to tell you. . . .

IMA
That's where your letters have been going.

HASKELL
Yes.

MILTON
And the money?

HASKELL
Every week.

MILTON
So you're bringing over a wife.

HASKELL
Yes.

MILTON
And you thought it'd just be a nice little surprise for us.

HASKELL
Mr. Perry, I want to tell you many times, but you keep giving me help and I owe you more and more money.

MILTON
You're damn right you do!

IMA
Milton, be careful.

MILTON
No, *you* be careful. I trusted you, son.

HASKELL
You can still trust.

MILTON
How many more of you are there?

HASKELL
Only my wife!

MILTON
Now, am I supposed to believe that?

(Pause.)

IMA
　You should have told us, Haskell.

HASKELL
　I tell you now.

MILTON
　When it's too late.

IMA
　Milton.

MILTON
　Well, our hands are tied. When does she get here?

HASKELL
　She's outside. In the wagon.

IMA
　Well, bring her in, Haskell. She's burning up out there.

HASKELL
(HE goes to the door and turns back.)
　You can rely on me, Mr. Perry. The risk is the same.

MILTON
　Yeah.

(HASKELL goes. As the PERRYs wait, we hear, "Zay vill'n dir bahkennen. Ich vill dos trog'n. Gib mir. Dos iss unzer neier krom. Vos klayost deh? Koom arein, fishele, koom arein." [They want to meet you. I'll carry that. Give

it here. This is our new shop. How do you like it? Come in, sweetie, come in.] HASKELL precedes HER, carrying HER belongings—wicker cases and clanking bundles. LEAH enters, clutching two candlesticks. SHE is small and frightened.)

HASKELL
My wife, Leah. Hob nit moireh, fishele. Zog eppes. Zog zeh gut morg'n. (Don't be afraid, sweetie. Say something. Tell them good morning.)

MILTON
Hello.

IMA
Hello.

(Immobile, SHE looks slowly at the PERRYs, at the store, at HASKELL. SHE opens HER mouth and is mute. HER panic grows and SHE becomes incapable of movement or speech. The only things SHE sees are HER candlesticks. The people and the room disappear and SHE is left alone.)

Scene Nine

Amid a jumble of sounds and voices, LEAH's travel clothing melts away and SHE is left in HER nightgown. It is several months later. HER candlesticks gleam as if with an inner light. SHE picks one up and seems not to recognize it.

LEAH
Och, mei' Gott, siz ah meshuggeneh velt. (Oh, my God, it's an insane world.)

HASKELL
(Offstage.)
Leah?

LEAH
Ah meshuggeneh velt.

HASKELL
(Entering.)
Leah, what are you doing?

LEAH
(Examining a candlestick.)
What is this?

HASKELL
What?

LEAH
What do I call this? Diese leichter.

HASKELL
It's a candlestick.

LEAH
> A candle shtick. A candle shtick. Ich verde meshuggeh.
> (I'm going insane.)

HASKELL
> Leah . . .

LEAH
> I'm stupid, Haskell.

HASKELL
> Leah, what's wrong? You're not stupid.

LEAH
> I am, yes. I'm stupid. Listen to me. F'n Aynglsh, I
> know ten words. I don't know what this is. A
> candle shtick. Mei' Gott.

HASKELL
> Leah, it's cold out here. Come back to bed.

LEAH
> I was at home always smart. I read. I could talk.

HASKELL
> Fishele, it takes time. It's hard.

LEAH
> Haskell, where are we?

HASKELL
> Where are we? We're at home. In our own place.

LEAH
> But where are *we*? Us.

71

HASKELL
(HE tries to usher HER from the room.)
Leah, come upstairs.

LEAH
Ich bin nit ah kint, Haskell.

HASKELL
I know you're not a child, Leah. . . .

LEAH
Something terrible's going to happen.

HASKELL
Leah, has someone treated you badly? Said something to you? Called you names?

LEAH
No, Haskell, no.

HASKELL
Well, I don't understand what . . .

LEAH
Look, Haskell! Look at this town! There must be thousands of places where we live.

HASKELL
Where we live?

LEAH
Where there are Jews.

HASKELL
Oh, Leah, please. We've talked about this . . .

LEAH

No. Nobody says things, but I walk down the street and I'm *so different*. People they come in, they stare at me. I can't help. I'm stupid. Are you so perfect? Don't this bother you, too?

HASKELL

Yes, of course, Leah, but what can we do?

LEAH

Let's leave, Haskell. Let's find our own people.

HASKELL

But, Leah, the store, our business . . .

LEAH

Yes, our business.

HASKEL

Leah, what the hell is happening?

LEAH

Look at you! Is your head covered? When did this stop? We don't eat kosher. . . .

HASKELL

Now, damn it, Leah!

LEAH

. . . we don't eat kosher, you don't pray at sundown . . .

HASKELL

What difference does that make, Leah?

73

LEAH
What difference? You're a Jew. I married a Jew.

HASKELL
I'm still a Jew! What, did I change in the night? Did I grow a tail? I know it's hard here, Leah . . .

LEAH
It's impossible.

HASKELL
It's not impossible. So we don't keep kosher. Where would we buy? My head is uncovered? I don't want to be strange, either. These people are our customers. They buy, we eat. Do you think God will hate me for that? Why does He need me to wear a little piece of cloth on my head? In twenty years, I'll wear a toupee, He'll be happy.

LEAH
Mei' Gott, you make a joke about it. It's nothing to you.

HASKELL
So what do you want, Leah? We should go back to Russia?

LEAH
No, Haskell, no.

HASKELL
Then what do you suggest we do?

LEAH
New York . . .

HASKELL
Never. I refuse.

LEAH
Tell me why.

HASKELL
Hester Street is a ghetto. They say the overcrowding is terrible. There's talk of cutting immigration altogether. *No.*

LEAH
Then there is no place for us.

HASKELL
Here is our place! I'm not going to run again! No more running! No more!! Our place is here! That's the *end! Yes?*

LEAH
(Pause.)
I'm alone. Mei' Gott, I'm alone.

(SHE stares at HIM for a long moment. SHE picks up HER candlesticks.)

I would polish these up, they could shine in the dark.

HASKELL
They're beautiful.

LEAH
Why? Two pieces of junk. Sell them, see what you can get.

HASKELL
Leah . . .

(SHE shoves them at HIM.)

LEAH
What is left? On Shabbos, I light the candles, you mumble a prayer. If being a Jew means owning two candlesticks then I don't want it. I don't want it! I don't want the baby! I don't want you!

HASKELL
(Silence.)
Leah. A baby?

LEAH
A baby, Haskell. We'll turn him loose like an animal.

HASKELL
No. No, no, no. Leah! A baby?!

LEAH
What do we do?

HASKELL
What do we do? Thank God! We rejoice!

(HE embraces HER.)

I don't see anything. When does it happen?

LEAH

Where will we go?

HASKELL

Leah. Mama. Do you know what I found out? Hamilton is only a little over fifty years old. Where did these people come from? You think Americans are only Americans. They, too, came from someplace else. Germany, Italy, China, everywhere. They were alone. Moses led the Israelites into a strange land.

LEAH

So now you're Moses?

HASKELL

I'm not Moses. I'm just saying, we're not the only ones.

LEAH

Haskell! I don't care about the past, who came from where. For my baby, there is no life here. Yes, of course. I can learn to live in a different house. I can learn a different language. I can say *howdy*, grow a cactus by the door. But my baby, Haskell, can't make these shortcuts. He can't grow up without God. To cover his head, do I buy a cowboy hat? Pointy boots, big belt buckle? He'd fit right in, huh?

HASKELL

Our baby won't be without God, Leah! This child will be a Jew. I don't know how. But when this person, this little Jewish person is born, we will have brought something new, something old into a different corner of the world. How many years have the Jews been wandering? Who says we can't wander to Texas and rest for a while?

LEAH
Yes, Moses.

(HASKELL sings the first verse of "Di Grine Kusine.")

It's like I never got off the boat.

(HE sings the second verse but SHE remains distant.)

I'm still looking for land.

ACT TWO

"The Chickens will Come Home to Roost"

SPECIAL SUBJECT OF

Come and
Hear
"JIMMIE"

Bring your
Chum
With You'

"*JIMMIE*" *SMITH*

SUNDAY NIGHT, 8:00 UNDER

Big Gospel Tent

OPPOSITE FIRST BAPTIST CHURCH

—AT—

Hamilton, Texas

Scene One

From the blackout, we hear the Calvary Baptist Church choir singing a vigorous version of "Where Shall I Be?" Lights come up on IMA in HER kitchen. SHE continues the hymn to HERSELF, preparing a vegetable stew. LEAH appears in the doorway, quite clearly nine months pregnant.

IMA

Oh! Leah! You scared me! What is it? Are you feeling all right?

LEAH

I was . . . tired, I guess.

IMA

Uh, are you . . . ?

LEAH

I'm not really tired. . . . I was . . . I wanted to go home but Haskell sent me over here.

IMA

Well . . . Why don't you . . . You want to lie down? You can use your old room.

LEAH

He told me to come help you.

IMA

Oh. Well . . . I've got a world of vegetables to get into this pot.

83

LEAH
I'm not much good.

IMA
What, honey?

LEAH
I'm stupid. I just . . .

IMA
Here you go.

(SHE gives HER an apron.)

Dora, would you just look at these carrots. One thing I'm sorry is Haskell let go of his grocery business. Somehow he always had the best things. Stuff you'd never seen before sometimes.

LEAH
His back is no good. The bags are too heavy. At home he never had to . . .

IMA
Well, he'll do right well with the new dry goods. He's a good businessman. We like him.

LEAH
I know.

IMA
(Handing HER a knife.)
Here. I'll cut and you skin.

84

(LEAH kisses HER right thumb, tucks it firmly into the apron's waistband, and takes the knife. Cutting with only HER left hand is clumsy. IMA grabs the carrot to steady it. LEAH cuts the end off, and IMA turns the carrot around. LEAH cuts the other end. IMA drops the trimmed carrot into the pot SHE's holding. There is a lonely plunk. THEY start on another carrot and a mockingbird calls from out the window.)

IMA
  Hello!

(As SHE reaches for the salt shaker, SHE knocks it over. Without thought, both women grab a pinch and toss it over THEIR shoulders in an identical fashion. THEY regard each other for a moment.)

  Just for luck, you know.

LEAH
  Yes. We do that, too.

IMA
  Well . . . luck is luck. Don't matter where, I guess. You got to laugh at that, though. Now why do you suppose it's going to do any good to throw more salt around after you've already spilled it? Seems like it'd be luckier to clean it up.

LEAH
  Maybe that's why they do it.

IMA
  That's why . . . what?

LEAH
  To clean it up.

(SHE scoops up the spilled salt and flings the whole mess over HER shoulder.)

IMA
  Well, you're most prob'ly right. Anyhow, we got good luck coming to us now.

LEAH
  Kenahoreh.

(SHE spits once—and hard.)

IMA
  What?

LEAH
  Oh. Nothing. It's . . .

IMA
  Oh. Well . . . all right.

LEAH
  Kenahoreh.

IMA
  Uh huh. Is that . . .?

LEAH
  Yiddish. Jewish. Kenahoreh. You say that to . . . when you don't want the . . . the evil eye.

IMA
    Honey, I hear you talking, but I'm stumped.

LEAH
    You said we got good luck coming to us and I said
    kenahoreh because it means no evil eye, because it's
    bad luck to wish for good luck. You'll attract the
    evil eye.

IMA
    Canorry.

LEAH
    Kenahoreh, that's right.

IMA
    Listen, I got one of those words, too.

LEAH
    You do?

IMA
    Padadooly.

LEAH
    What does it mean?

IMA
    I have no earthly idea. My mama was a very super-
    stitious woman. I'd hear it a dozen times a day.

LEAH
    Padadooly.

IMA
  I don't know what's supposed to happen when you
  say it. Nothing, I 'spect, if it's working. Well, in
  fact, you wanna see something superstitious, you
  looky here.

*(From behind the hem of her apron, SHE reveals HER
talisman.)*

LEAH
  What is it?

IMA
  Well, it's a rabbit's foot.

LEAH
  Really?

IMA
  Well, yes. *(SHE recites.)*

  Do not depend on a
    rabbit's foot
  Nor get your hopes up
    too soon
  Unless it is the left
    hind one
  And was caught by the
    light of the moon.

'Course I don't know if this'n's regulation or not, it's
been so long. Still, it might be the left hind one.
What do you think?

LEAH
   Yes. That's why I do this.

(SHE kisses and tucks HER thumb as before.)

IMA
   So you don't get the . . . canary.

LEAH
   Kenahoreh—that's right.

IMA
   Well, Dora—if I didn't wonder.

LEAH
   I've never . . . This is my first . . .

IMA
   Honey, you just go right ahead.

LEAH
   No, I mean . . . I was scared. And . . . I'm not so
   scared now.

IMA
   Scared of what?

(SHE reads LEAH's face.)

   Oh, Dora! Not me! Well, I got to laugh at that.
   There's not enough to me to be scared of.

(SHE touches the crucifix at HER neck.)

I'm a Christian?

(A distant, ghostlike balalaika is heard.)

LEAH
When I was little, in Bobruysk, most of my friends
were Gentile. We lived near a Catholic church and
we play there and run around and who knew the
difference? Once a priest walked by in his black
cassock and black hat and his beard and he didn't
look no different from the rabbi. To me. And my
friends, they ran up to him and kissed his ring. So
what do I do? I don't want to be left out, so I ran up
to him and kneeled down and kissed his ring and he
patted my head and my mother gave me the worst
beating of my life. Someone would put up a sign.
"Brothers in Christ! If you love Holy Mother Russia, you will get rid of the Jews!" I love Mother
Russia, too. I don't want to be afraid of you. You're
nice. It's . . .

(A mockingbird sings. SHE looks for it.)

What is that one?

IMA
That's our mockingbird.

LEAH
Mocking bird.

IMA
I come a good piece myself. Not so far as you, but
pretty far.

LEAH
You're not from Hamilton?

IMA
Dorena, Missouri. A little bitty river town on the Mississippi—and made to get out of, let me tell you. My papa was the first to go. He ran off barefooted after Mama buried his shoes and wouldn't tell him where.

LEAH
She buried his shoes?

IMA
Well, if your husband's sorta light-foot, as they say, you take and bury his shoes somewhere near the house and he'll stay home. Least till he finds 'em. She did the same thing with our dogs.

LEAH
She buried their shoes?

IMA
She cut off the tips of their tails. Buried 'em under the back porch. Now that seemed to work. She never let me sleep with a doll. Said it'd dance on my head in the night and make me crazy. Dora! I tell you who was the crazy woman. Hamilton, Texas, still wasn't far enough away from her.

LEAH
It's far away for me.

IMA
Well . . .

LEAH
  I loved my mama.

IMA
  Well, I did, too, honey, but it was such a backwards
  life.

LEAH
  I'd hang on to her. Really. Hang on to her dress
  while she was cooking or . . . and she would send
  me outside, but I'd sneak around to the window so I
  could just watch her.

IMA
  Well, that's silly. You should go out and play.

LEAH
  Do you have children, Ima?

IMA
  No. Well, yes, of course. Now why did I say that? I
  had two boys. I lost one early on and the other,
  Charlie, is . . . left home. Left his crazy ol' mama
  behind. Like I left mine. Well, if I didn't forget
  the onions. There's just no flavor at all without
  the onions.

(Pause.)

LEAH
  You know, I can't believe she cut the tails off those . . .

IMA
  Those dogs? Oh, Dora! Our neighbor? Her husband

got the TB, so she tried to make up a tonic for him
where you had to boil down a live dog.

LEAH

The dogs had a pretty hard time there!

IMA

No, you didn't want to be a dog in Dorena. Now
some of those old superstitions there was some sense
to. Like I remember she'd never let us eat fish and
milk together. Now that'll make you sick.

LEAH

We have that!

IMA

You do?

LEAH

Well, sort of like that. We don't eat milk and meat
together. I mean, we used not to.

IMA

Did it make you sick?

LEAH

No. It's not kosher.

IMA

What's that?

LEAH

Kosher? It's certain foods that you can't eat.

IMA
Well, you see? It's the same thing.

LEAH
No, it's not the same at all! It's in our Torah. It's
the Jewish law. I mean, yours was superstition but
ours, keeping kosher, is . . . was our religion.

IMA
And you don't do it no more.

LEAH
No. Well, yes, some . . . if I can, but . . . but it's
not superstition. We *believe* that. But I don't understand Haskell. He's so quick to say we've got to
change, we've got to change, it's not possible here.
If it's something you believe, you can't just throw it
away. It's part of you. And once that is gone, what
am I? And what will my . . . ?

(SHE tries to withhold HER tears.)

IMA
Well, these're strong onions, aren't they?

LEAH
Yeah.

IMA
Now, you're gonna laugh at this. Take a piece of the
outside skin. Take one.

(SHE does.)

And put it on your head. Do it.

(SHE does.)

Now that'll keep it from burning your eyes. Is it working?

LEAH
No.

IMA
All right, I got one more. Mama always had a backup. No, leave that there. And hold this matchstick between your teeth. Now say padadooly three times.

(SHE does.)

Is it working?

(LEAH shakes HER head.)

Well, a lot of those old notions—just hocus pocus . . . just plain hot air.

LEAH
If it's nothing but hot air, how come you still wear that rabbit leg?

IMA
Well, I wouldn't want to be foolish, child.

(LEAH, finally unable to withhold HER tears, weeps bitterly. IMA, also unable to withhold HERSELF, lightly

touches HER arm and LEAH rushes to HER, cradling HERSELF in IMA's breast.)

Honey, some things you just don't let go of.

(LEAH rocks HERSELF in IMA's arms, humming "Di Grine Kusine.")

What's that you're singing?

LEAH
When I get upset, Haskell sings it to me to calm me down. It works better when he does it.

IMA
Sing it.

LEAH
It's about a girl who comes to America. Red cheeks and dancing feet and all she learns is to stop dancing. She don't have such a very good time.

IMA
Sing it.

(LEAH timidly begins singing the song. SHE takes IMA's hands and THEY start to dance in a little circle. As HER enthusiasm grows, LEAH's face begins to glow. By the second verse, SHE begins to sing full voice. Suddenly, SHE is contorted by the first of HER major contractions. IMA goes to HER and puts HER arms around HER.)

IMA
Well, honey, it's about time.

Scene Two

The Harelik front porch, late that night. LEAH's cries are heard from within. HASKELL paces the porch. HE calls inside.

HASKELL
  Ima? Miz Perry?

IMA
(Offstage.)
  Yes, Haskell, what is it?

HASKELL
  Is she all right? I called Dr. Cleveland over an hour ago. I don't know what's taking him so long.

IMA

  (SHE comes to the door.)

  He's in here, Haskell. You let him in some time ago.

HASKELL
  I did?

IMA
  Yes.

HASKELL
  Oh, good. How is Leah?

IMA
  She's fine. Listen, Haskell, you want us all to come out on the porch? We could talk a lot easier that way.

THE IMMIGRANT

(MILTON appears at the edge of the yard.)

Milton!

(SHE goes to HIM. In a whisper.)

What took you so long? He's like to turn inside out.

MILTON
All right, I'll set with him.

IMA
I should hope so!

(SHE goes back to the porch.)

Whyn't y'all visit for a spell. It might be *very relaxing.*

(SHE goes in. Silence.)

MILTON
The place looks good, Haskell.

HASKELL
Mm hmm.

MILTON
You're quite a gardener.

HASKELL
What?

MILTON
You're quite a gardener. The place looks good.

HASKELL
Well, it's not me. Leah plants the garden.

MILTON
Well, I don't mean just . . . I mean . . . the *bushes* and things. That magnolia's really taking hold. Damnation!

(The porch step has nearly dumped HIM onto the ground.)

This step is awful loose, Haskell.

HASKELL
Oh, I know. I put a couple bricks there, but they slip out.

MILTON
Well, a hammer and two nails would keep it in place before somebody breaks their neck!

(A sharp cry is heard from LEAH.)

HASKELL
Ima! What was that? It sounded real bad!

IMA
(Offstage.)
Haskell . . .

HASKELL
Is she all right?

IMA
(Coming to the door.)

Haskell, would you relax? She's fine.

HASKELL
I'm relaxed. Does she have to scream?

IMA
Listen, Haskell, would you like to come in and help for a while? Hold her hand or something?

HASKELL
Yes! Of course I will!

IMA
Just keep the noise down.

HASKELL
Excuse me, Milton. They need me for a minute. Relax.

MILTON
I'll be all right here.

(IMA and HASKELL exit. Another cry from LEAH is heard. THEY emerge again, HASKELL reeling.)

IMA
Here, bend your head over. Breathe through your nose. Sit. Stay.

(To MILTON.)

He'll be more help out here. Keep him quiet.

(SHE goes into the house. A mockingbird sings.)

MILTON
You're waking up the whole neighborhood here.
You know, if you whistle at it, a mockingbird will
pick up your tune and sing it back to you? You
wanna give it a . . . ? Here. Listen.

*(HE whistles. The bird sings something entirely different.
HE tries a different whistle. The bird sings something different again.)*

See? Haskell, you thought about a name?

HASKELL
Matleh.

MILTON
Mm hmm. That a boy or a girl?

HASKELL
Girl.

MILTON
Yeah, I figured it was. It's nice.

HASKELL
Yes. My grandmother, may she rest in peace.

MILTON
Yes, indeed. And if it's a . . .

HASKELL
Mordechai.

MILTON
Oh, that's a good one. Relative?

HASKELL
No, Bible.

MILTON
Ah.

HASKELL
He was an uncle of Esther.

MILTON
Now which one is she?

HASKELL
Queen Esther! Saved the ancient Jews from Haman.

(LEAH cries.)

MILTON
(Calls across the street.)
Hello, Miz Castle! . . . No, everything's fine. . . .
No, no trouble. We just got a loose step here.

(Muttering.)

Yeah, we'll get a man right on it.

(A baby's cry is heard.)

HASKELL
I can't stand it! My God! When will it stop?

MILTON
Haskell.

HASKELL
  I can't take this!

MILTON
  Have a cigar!

(The baby is heard again from within.)

HASKELL
  Leah!

(Runs inside.)

IMA
(Offstage.)
  Haskell!

(At the door, HASKELL nearly runs IMA down.)

IMA
  Oh!

(SHE sits, exhausted.)

  A boy. She's fine.

MILTON
(Also sitting.)
  You made it just in time.

IMA
  How'd you manage to keep him in his skin?

MILTON
  Bird imitations.

HASKELL
(Banging through with a bundle.)
  Excuse me, please.

(HE places the baby in the middle of the yard.)

IMA
  What in the world are you doing?!

HASKELL
  Put the baby on the ground.

IMA
  What?

HASKELL
  Touch the baby to the ground for good luck.

IMA
  Well, pick it up! It's been there long enough!

HASKELL
  Mordechai. Welcome to America.

MILTON
  Esther's uncle.

IMA
  Esther who?

Scene Three

The scene is the same—late at night, four years later. MIL-
TON is in the porch chair. HASKELL is at the door, as
LEAH's cries are heard from within. THEY share a look as
HASKELL passes MILTON and moves into the yard.

MILTON
Well, I'll tell you one thing. This young Doc Cleveland is a damn sight more reliable than his daddy.
You know Charlie, our youngest, come all by himself? I'd run my fool head off to fetch *old* Doc
Cleveland and by the time we got back Charlie was
just settin' there looking at us. And that old fart
charged me for the full delivery just the same.

(HE steps on the same bad step and it gives way as before).

Goddamn it, Haskell, haven't you ever fixed this
thing?

HASKELL
Oh. We always use the other side.

MILTON
Jesus Christ, son! And you with a pregnant wife
walking up and down this thing twenty times a day.

HASKELL
Yes, I'm sorry. I should fix it. Those bricks slip out.

MILTON
Look. Look here. This whole piece is busted out—

HASKELL
I know it's busted. That's why I put the bricks—

MILTON
—and the support in the back is settin' on its side.

HASKELL
Yes, I'm sorry!

MILTON
Well hell!!

IMA
(At the door.)
Would you two quiet down out here? I'd shut the door, but she says it'd keep the angels from helping the baby, so you're just gonna have to pipe down.

HASKELL
How is she?

IMA
She's working hard. She's fine. Now *hush up!*

(IMA exits.)

MILTON
Sometimes that voice irritates the hell outta me. You talk about something to vibrate your skull. Ima's Cavalry Baptist. Wednesday nights and twice on Sunday. She got me to go a couple of times, but I tell you, everybody *in* there's got a voice like that.

107

HASKELL
Miz Castle came into the store today, said she was praying for us and our poor children.

MILTON
How's that?

HASKELL
Well, I guess she's Church of Christ and the whole congregation is concerned about these unbaptized children being born.

MILTON
Yeah, well, bunch of do-gooders out stirring up some good to do. Ima's been raggin' *my* butt to get baptized. Used to, she didn't bring it up so often, but the older we get . . .

HASKELL
Why is it so . . .

MILTON
Important? Why, you'll go to hell, son. Straight to hell.

HASKELL
Sounds bad.

MILTON
Sounds about the *same*, if you ask me.

(A sharp cry from LEAH pulls HASKELL's attention.)

Got a name picked out?

HASKELL
Well, if it's a girl, Matleh.

MILTON
Oh, yeah . . .

HASKELL
My grandmother.

MILTON
Your grandmother, that's right.

HASKELL
And a boy would be Moishe.

MILTON
Moishe.

HASKELL
It's Yiddish for Moses.

MILTON
Mordechai, Matley, Moishe . . . You're gonna give
Church of Christ the fits.

IMA
(In the doorway, smiling.)
Haskell!

HASKELL
Oh, my God! So soon?

IMA
So soon? Well, we got bored in there and . . .

(HE rushes past HER.)

. . . all right, hold on, Haskell, I know where you're headed.

(As SHE spreads the quilt SHE's holding on the ground, HASKELL dashes out with the baby. SHE guides HIM to the quilt.)

I don't know why y'all insist on this. It can't be good for the child.

HASKELL
Moishe.

MILTON
Another unbaptized Texan.

111

Scene Four

The scene is the same—late at night, three years later. LEAH's cries are heard. Discovered are HASKELL and MILTON on their hands and knees at the porch steps. A blanket is spread on the lawn. MILTON pounds away with a hammer.

MILTON
Okay, now, I think that fits.

Got another nail?

(It is hammered into place.)

Now, by God, I think she'll do.

(MILTON backs off and steps on the same place as before. It gives way as before.)

God . . . bless America! All right now, what the hell happened?

IMA
(Appearing at the door.)
All right now, look. I can't shut the door 'cause it'd keep the angels away, so you're gonna have to stop construction.

MILTON
Well, never mind, Haskell. We can prop it up with these bricks.

IMA
Why're you doing this in the middle of the night, anyways?

MILTON
It needed fixing!

IMA
Dora!

(SHE exits. MILTON stands on the step, testing it. It holds.)

MILTON
I believe bricks is the answer, Haskell. You're gonna get a much solider base with these bricks under here.

HASKELL
Milton, have you tried one of my jujubes?

(HE runs to the edge of the stage and back, having picked two small fruits.)

MILTON
One of your what?

HASKELL
Jujubes. I planted this when Morty was born, but it's taken this long to make anything out of it. Here, taste it.

MILTON
Looks like a date.

HASKELL
It's a desert fruit. They grow them in Palestine. We have this tradition to plant trees. Someone is born, you plant a tree. Someone dies, you plant a tree. Someone plants a tree, you plant a tree. Now, the jujube is for Mordechai. That plum tree is for Moishe. And I'll have something for this one. They say it's to show a faith in the future. Children and trees—they take a long time to grow into something, so you must have faith in the future.

MILTON
Sure. You hold a baby in your arms and you think everything's gonna turn out blue skies. Our Charlie? Out battin' around from one skunk-hole to another? Just turned on me. Run off.

HASKELL
(Pause.)
I ran away.

MILTON
Yes, but . . . !

HASKELL
Well, I left my parents. May they rest in peace, I practically left them to die. But I saw everyone growing twisted and for my children I want something else. I'm glad I left but I'm sorry I ran.

MILTON
Hell, you're sittin' pretty. You got family. Your kids are too young to turn on you.

(A baby is heard from within. The men stand.)

IMA
(Appearing on the porch with a bundled baby.)
　　All right, Haskell, come a'runnin'!

(SHE hands HIM the bundle.)

　　Three boys in a row.

MILTON
　　Well, damn. Your grandmother's gonna be mighty
　　disappointed.

HASKELL
　　She's been dead fifty years. She can take it.

(HE hands MILTON the bundle.)

　　Quick, put him on the ground.

MILTON
　　Wait! Now hold on a minute. Isn't that your job?

HASKELL
　　Special circumstances.

MILTON
　　What circumstances?

IMA
　　Honey, they've named him Milton.

MILTON
  Well, that's too bad. You've gone and ruined him
  for sure.

(HE places the baby on the quilt.)

HASKELL
  It's another boy, Miz Castle! . . . No, she's been
  expecting for the last nine months. . . . Yes, I'm
  sure of it. Will you come see him tomorrow? . . .
  Wonderful . . . Thank you!

*(He turns to look back at the PERRYs with his baby
boy.)*

  Thank you.

Scene Five

1939. LEAH is discovered at the HARELIK dinner table set for the Sabbath meal. The silver candlesticks and the wine glasses gleam. Two loaves of challah rest beneath their ceremonial cover. HASKELL, IMA, and MILTON are gathered upstage as though in another room. LEAH places a kerchief on HER head, lights the two candles, and recites the blessing beneath HER breath. SHE removes the kerchief and calls out.

LEAH
  Haskell, everybody! Supper!

(HASKELL, IMA, and MILTON come into the room. To HASKELL.)

  Good Shabbos. We couldn't wait.

HASKELL
  Oh, sweetie, I'm sorry.

(Kissing HER.)

  Good Shabbos.

(The greetings are exchanged with IMA and MILTON.)

LEAH
  That means "Have a good Sabbath."

IMA
  Like Merry Christmas.

LEAH
  That's right.

MILTON
  Haskell, did we hold you up here?

HASKELL
  No, no, no. Shabbos starts at sundown, so we have
  to light the candles before it gets dark.

IMA
  You still have those beautiful candlesticks, honey.

LEAH
  Oh, no! I'm not letting go of these!

HASKELL
(Indicates HER seat.)
  Ima, please.

MILTON
  So the day doesn't start in the morning?

HASKELL
  No, the day starts at night.

LEAH
(Indicates HIS seat.)
  Milton . . .

HASKELL
  I mean, the day . . . not the day but the beginning . . .

(HE looks to LEAH for help.)

LEAH
  Our holidays begin at sunset. When the sun sets, it
  completes the old day.

119

(LEAH has two skullcaps. SHE hands one to HASKELL and HE puts it on.)

HASKELL
  It completes the old day, that's right. I mean, the morning is still the morning.

MILTON
  Well, that's a relief.

HASKELL
  That's a relief, so good Shabbos.

(LEAH silently asks HASKELL if SHE should offer MIL-TON the second skullcap. HE shakes HIS head and pockets it.)

  Now the first thing is the blessing for the children.

LEAH
  Who aren't here.

HASKELL
  We bless them anyway. They need it.

LEAH
  They all left to go deer hunting with the Tolberts. I don't know.

MILTON
  Oh, Tolbert'll keep a good eye on 'em. They've got a real nice stand down near Lampasas.

LEAH
  I like them to go, get outside, but . . .

HASKELL
Milton pesters us to buy a gun. All their friends have guns. You say no, but . . .

LEAH
Oh! And cars. If they can tear all over the place in someone's car, oh! Heaven! And little Milton is the worst.

(MILTON rejoices.)

HASKELL
Milton's not the worst.

(Together.)

LEAH	HASKELL
(To IMA.) Seventeen years old, he goes out, he stays late.	All right, we're getting off the track here.

HASKELL
All right, the children.

(HE recites the blessing.)

Now, in English it means . . . it says to grow up strong and wise and the Lord turn His face to you and give you peace.

IMA
That is just amazing. I'm so glad we're doing this!

LEAH
Oh, I am, too. It's really perfect. The kids are away. We don't hardly see you no more.

IMA
  I know it.

HASKELL
  Now, this prayer is called the Kiddush. It's the blessing of the Sabbath.

IMA
  Shabbos.

LEAH
  That's right.

IMA
  It's such a pretty word.

MILTON
  All right, quiet now. Let the man do his business.

(HASKELL recites the Kiddush.)

LEAH
  Now we say omayn here, but it's the same thing as
  amen, so . . .

(THEY say it.)

HASKELL
  Now this means "Blessed are You, O Lord God,
  King of the Universe. You gave us the command-
  ments, you, uh . . .

LEAH
  ". . . You gave us the holy Shabbos to remind us of

the Creation, to remind us of our liberation from Egypt; we who are Your chosen people . . ." Oh . . .

HASKELL
There were a lot fewer people then, I think. It was an easier choice.

LEAH
"Blessed are You, O Lord God, Who makes the Sabbath holy."

MILTON
All right now. That's very nice.

HASKELL
And we drink the wine.

(IMA balks.)

MILTON
Oh now, Ima. I think this'd be an exception, don't you?

IMA
(To HASKELL and LEAH.)
Well, now, I'm embarrassed, I guess. Baptist Church doesn't drink. Ever.

LEAH
Oh, honey! I didn't even think of that. Of course, it's all right. Here, give me the glass. Maybe some fruit juice . . .

IMA
Oh, now I feel bad. I just hate to insult your beautiful little ceremony.

HASKELL
Ima, it's no insult.

IMA
I'll make an exception.

LEAH
No, no.

IMA
I'll make an exception. Now, this is just between us and the candlesticks.

(SHE raises the glass.)

All right then, down the hatch or whatever.

MILTON
I don't think "down the hatch" is quite what's called for.

HASKELL
L'Chaim.

MILTON
L'okay . . .

LEAH
To Life. L'Chaim.

ALL
  L'Chaim.

MILTON
  And many more.

HASKELL
  Yes, sir.

(THEY drink.)

IMA
  Ooh! That's strong! It's good, though. I mean the
  aftertaste is very . . .

(MILTON is smirking.)

  Oh, hush up.

HASKELL
  And the last blessing is for the bread.

*(HE uncovers the two shining loaves of challah. HE recites
the blessing and passes pieces to all.)*

LEAH
  You have to break it off, because if you cut it with a
  knife . . .

IMA
  You get the canary.

LEAH
  Right.

HASKELL
Blessed is the Lord God, King of the Universe . . .
uh . . .

LEAH
Who brings forth the bread from the earth.

HASKELL
Thank you, professor. Good Shabbos, everybody.
Now let's eat.

LEAH
All right! There's the bowls. Haskell, serve the
borscht. There's bread and butter and here are . . .

(SHE uncovers the serving dish.)

. . . the blintzes!

MILTON
Uh huh.

LEAH
Now don't look for the meat. These are all cheese.

MILTON
So it's just . . . what is it?

LEAH
Oh! It's blintzes.

(SHE serves two to MILTON.)

A blintz.

Two blintzes.

MILTON
A blintz.

LEAH
It's from the old country.

HASKELL
They're delicious.

LEAH
You see, they're like real thin kind of pancakes
wrapped around this sweet cheese.

MILTON
Sweet cheese.

IMA
Well, I don't think we've ever come across . . .

LEAH
Now here's applesauce, here's sour cream. You can
mix a little or just separate, either way.

MILTON
And this is . . .

HASKELL
Borscht.

LEAH
Spinach borscht.

MILTON
Borscht.

LEAH
It's a cold soup.

IMA
Oh! Well, that fresh dill smells delicious.

LEAH
So, eat.

HASKELL
Now, Milton, I want you to try this blintz with a
little applesauce on it.

(HE spoons some onto MILTON's blintz.)

MILTON
Is that good on there?

HASKELL
It's delicious. Now you just taste it.

MILTON
Applesauce on the blintz. Okay . . .

(MILTON gives it a try as everyone watches.)

Well, that's good. Leah, that's delicious.

HASKELL
Now will you relax? They're fine. All day she's been
worrying.

LEAH
Well, on Shabbos we like to eat just dairy, so I didn't know.

IMA
(Having sampled the borscht.)
Well, honey, this is just delicious. I mean it. It's real good.

LEAH
Oh, thank you. It's still strange, to have so much meat. Every day, practically.

HASKELL
Because in the old country we'd get a chicken, sleep with it for a week, we were so happy.

IMA
It must have just been awful.

HASKELL
There's no word to say how it was. Was it awful? You fear for your life. Oh, yes. All the time. And with another monster on the loose in Europe, it's hard to stop thinking about it.

LEAH
Ooh, when I think of that Milton yesterday . . . I haven't seen you that angry in years.

IMA
What'd he do this time?

LEAH
We were listening to the radio and all of a sudden,

OUR WINDOWS TELL YOU OF FASHION'S LATEST DECREES

FORWARD WITH HAMILTON
SINCE 1911

HASKELL HARELIK DRY GOODS COMPANY

the music stops and we hear this announcement and they say that Hitler is dead. That somebody got into his headquarters and killed him.

MILTON
You heard this yesterday?

HASKELL
We were crying and laughing and dancing around. We couldn't believe it. And then by accident I knock over the radio and what do I see? Two little wires. And where do these two little wires lead? The kids' bedroom.

LEAH
They had hooked up this microphone to have some fun with us.

HASKELL
Microphone!

LEAH
Hitler is dead. Haskell took his belt after them.

HASKELL
But the frightening thing is they thought it was funny.

MILTON
Well, those boys'll find a joke in just about anything.

HASKELL
Yes, but I mean, to them there is no danger. They are safe. Whatever is happening is far away—oceans

away and so they make a joke. It scares me. Not just
my sons, but most people I think.

MILTON
Most people what?

HASKELL
Think they are safe.

MILTON
Where?

HASKELL
Here.

LEAH
Now, Haskell, mach nit a gantsen tsimmes. (Don't
make a big deal.)

HASKELL
Who's making a tsimmes? We're just talking.

MILTON
What exactly are we in danger from, Haskell?

HASKELL
There's Hitler, there's Mussolini.

(Together.)

LEAH	MILTON
He's very angry about it.	You're talking about a real localized conflict there.

132

IMA
Well, he's talking to the original conservative.

HASKELL
How can you say it's localized? It involves all of Europe.

MILTON
Then it's a real European conflict. We're a long ways off from there, Haskell.

HASKELL
Not as far as you think, Milton.

MILTON
You stick your nose into other people's business and you're gonna get it whacked off. There's no reason to involve the rest of the planet.

HASKELL
(To IMA.)
Am I involving the rest of the planet?

IMA
Dora! Don't drag me into this. I don't know nothing about it.

LEAH
It's just a frightening thing, Mr. Perry. They say thousands are being killed.

MILTON
Now wait just a second. Let's not work it around so I have to defend these bastards. Excuse me. The

only reason I'm on about this is you know Roosevelt is trying to involve us in this thing and I think it would be the biggest mistake.

HASKELL
You think it's a big *mistake*, it *still* might be the best thing to do.

MILTON
That's right. Raise taxes and start wars.

HASKELL
Finish wars.

MILTON
Same difference.

IMA
Maybe you two would like to settle this out in the yard?

HASKELL
Milton, you're just like the kids with the radio. There's nothing bad happening here, so why worry? We'll wait till they're at the city limits. Maybe Mr. Tolbert'll loan us a deer rifle.

MILTON
Oh, Haskell.

HASKELL
Well . . .

IMA

It's a savage world, I guess. Makes life in Hamilton seem awful quiet.

LEAH

I love it here. I would never leave.

(THEY eat in silence for a bit, then . . .)

(Together.)

HASKELL	MILTON
The reason it's quiet is the world stops at the city limits.	Hamilton is quiet because we've managed to avoid getting into everyone else's business.

HASKELL

Milton, you have to put some of your concern out into the world.

MILTON

Haskell, what the hell are you on about? You're an American now.

IMA

Milton, don't start something. . . .

MILTON

May I talk, please? You don't live there anymore. You're here. Forget about it.

HASKELL

I can't forget.

MILTON

You've been here thirty years!

HASKELL
They're my people.

MILTON
Then why didn't you stay there and fight? Why did you have to run off?

(*There is a stunned silence.*)

IMA
He didn't mean it like that.

MILTON
Don't apologize for me.

HASKELL
Because we were being killed off, Milton. We had no way to fight back.

(*Silence.*)

IMA
We're very lucky to have you here.

HASKELL
And we're lucky to be here, Ima. It almost sounds like an accident, doesn't it?

MILTON
An accident.

LEAH
Haskell, it's not an accident. It's God's blessing.

MILTON
Haskell, I seem to remember you had some help along the way.

136

HASKELL

Milton, I don't forget that. I'm not ungrateful. But after a while, after many years, in fact, of accepting gifts and giving thanks, instead of filling you up, it makes you smaller. You have to be able to give back. This is what fills you up. And the one thing I would most like to give, I can't.

IMA

What is that, Haskell?

HASKELL

Freedom. Share my freedom with my own people. As an American.

MILTON

Where would you put them?

HASKELL

My God, Milton, what is all this land, this space around us? The wealth is embarrassing.

MILTON

Well, how long would that continue to be the case if we brought in a million, two million starving people every year. Would you hand out credit to every person who walked in your store?

HASKELL

No, but Milton . . .

MILTON

It's very sad, Haskell, but it can't be done.

HASKELL

Thirty years ago maybe half a million Jews came here every year—

MILTON
Along with the ghettos and crowded slums . . .

HASKELL
. . . and last year they let in five thousand refugees from Eastern Europe. Five thousand.

(Together.)

MILTON	HASKELL
Five thousand, fine. Five million, no.	*(To IMA.)* Does that sound like the doors are open?

IMA
I think we ought not to talk politics if it's the Sabbath.

LEAH
Haskell, she's right.

HASKELL
Doesn't fix anything to say you can't talk about it.

MILTON
All right, now, wait a second. Let's not forget you cost me a lot of money before you cleared your debts.

(Together.)

LEAH	IMA
Mr.Perry!	Milton!

MILTON
Now, wait a second! . . . and I was happy to do it.

But if there had been two of you or *more*, a man would have to stop and think about it, now wouldn't he?

HASKELL
In other words, you're only ready to help somebody if it's easy.

MILTON
You're calling me a selfish man, and I resent that, goddamn it. Only a fool would carry generosity to the point of stupidity. You wouldn't run your business like that.

HASKELL
This isn't business, Milton! It's people. We could provide for more than five thousand people a year. Any child could figure that. They don't have to crowd into Hester Street. They don't have to get on relief. I didn't.

MILTON
Well, you're an exceptional case, Haskell.

HASKELL
I'm not a case, Milton, I'm a person. . . .

(Together.)

LEAH
Haskell, you're being silly. It's Shabbos, for God's sake.

HASKELL
. . . and I'm not exceptional, I'm normal.

HASKELL (Continued)
I'm the same as everybody trying to get in. If I were immigrating today, I wouldn't even pass Customs. They demand a literacy test now. They demand only skilled laborers. No, the fact is, the United States is a castle. The moat on one side is the Pacific Ocean; the other side is the Atlantic. And the suffering of people? A rumor in the newspaper.

MILTON
So what are all we rich, lazy Americans supposed to do?

HASKELL
Open the doors a little. Take a position in the world.

MILTON
Enter the war.

HASKELL
If we must, yes.

MILTON
Haskell, you sound like a broken record. I appreciate your sympathy for your people. Fact of the matter is, there's a lot more than Jews having trouble way out there beyond that moat. But you can only do so much. Things are not equal in this world, Haskell.

HASKELL
Oh, Milton!

MILTON
Maybe we are a castle, but it makes damn little sense to tear it apart just because it's the only one.

HASKELL
Milton, that kind of talk makes me ashamed. And this in a so-called Christian country.

LEAH
Shah! Haskell!

MILTON
Well, we'd best be going.

IMA
Oh, honey, now please. Let's just change the subject.

MILTON
I'll be damned if I'm going to sit here and be called a miser and especially by you. Where the hell would you be if it wasn't for me?

HASKELL
I'm not a beggar, Milton.

MILTON
Nobody has ever given me a goddamn thing.

IMA
That's not true, Milton.

MILTON
So if I want to live in peace and quiet without turning over the keys to every damn stray dog, what the hell business is it of yours?

HASKELL
Go on, then! Go live your life.

MILTON
  Come on.

HASKELL
  You've helped me. I'm grateful. Why should you do anything more?

MILTON
  Ima! Let's *go!*

(HE leaves.)

IMA
  I really think I oughta . . .

LEAH
  No, Ima, please don't. I'm fine. I promise. I'll talk to you. I'm so sorry.

HASKELL
(After THEY've gone.)
  I've paid my debt to you! I don't owe you a goddamn thing!

(In a fury, HE blows out the candles.)

Scene Six

The HARELIK front porch, the following spring. HASKELL is replacing some loose slats in the porch railing. LEAH enters from the street with three bolts of red cloth.

LEAH
Well, the cloth came for the graduation gowns.

HASKELL
Oh, good. Finally.

LEAH
I was afraid we didn't order enough, but Jimmy Wiley's being held back a grade, so there's just enough.

HASKELL
Who's working on them? Are you going to have it by Sunday?

LEAH
We'll have it. It's all arranged.

HASKELL
All right.

LEAH
I thought Ima might like to help out since Milton's graduating.

HASKELL
You should ask her.

LEAH
  I did.

HASKELL
  Oh, good.

LEAH
  I just saw her down at the square. She didn't know
  he was graduating. I was embarrassed for her, Haskell.

HASKELL
  Well, we should invite them.

LEAH
  You know Milton can't go.

HASKELL
  Well, invite Ima then.

LEAH
  She scared me. I don't think she gets out anymore.

HASKELL
  Leah, if you want to invite Ima to the graduation
  then do it. You don't need my permission.

LEAH
  What do *you* want, Haskell?

HASKELL
  I'd like to finish this before midnight so the house
  won't fall down—if I could.

LEAH
  She asked if you would come over.

HASKELL
Well, we should sometime.

LEAH
She asked for tonight.

HASKELL
I don't think so.

LEAH
Why?

HASKELL
I just don't think it's a good idea.

LEAH
Why?

(HE works in silence.)

You don't have an answer.

HASKELL
I don't have an answer because it's not worth discussing, Leah.

LEAH
It's not worth it that Ima is frightened and alone in that house with a very sick man?

HASKELL
Please, Leah, I'm sorry for that, too. But Milton and I are different people. We're different from each

THE IMMIGRANT

other. We're different from what we were. It's best
to recognize that.

LEAH
And you should also recognize that what you're
doing is the same as running away. Isn't it, Haskell?

(HE works in silence.)

You don't have an answer.

(SHE goes in the house.)

146

Scene Seven

The PERRY front porch, that evening. A radio plays next to MILTON's old rocker.

ANNOUNCER
. . . And here's a little reminder from Haskell Harelik's Department Store in Hamilton that it's not too late to remember the graduate in *your* family. This week, they're featuring those good Red Goose Foot Builder shoes. . . . And for the girl grad, they've got those class year anklet socks she's been asking about, with her graduating year monogrammed right on the top.

(IMA comes out from the house and looks down the street.)

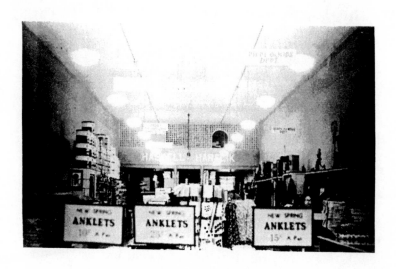

THE IMMIGRANT

So if you want to come in and browse or just get out of the heat, I know ol' Haskell is always glad to see you. That's the word from Haskell Harelik's on the south side of the square in Hamilton.

(Texas swing music begins playing and continues until the radio is shut off. We hear a car pull up. IMA waves.)

IMA
(Calling inside the house.)
　They're here, hon! Hey, y'all, hello!

LEAH
(Offstage.)
　Hello!

(We hear the slam of a car door.)

IMA
　Haskell, you can park around by the well, that'll be fine.

(LEAH enters.)

So, come on up. All right, well, here we are.

(LEAH hands HER a wicker basket.)

IMA
　Oh now, what's this?

LEAH
　Bagels.

IMA
　Oh, I was hoping it was *bagels*! That last batch you

148

made? We went through it in about a day, I'll swan if we didn't.

LEAH
(A Mason jar is also in the basket.)
    And this is plum jelly from our trees.

IMA
    Oh, now you're making me feel bad. You didn't have to bring anything.

LEAH
    Oh, hush.

IMA
    Well, come on up.

(HASKELL enters, but holds back.)

    I thought we'd set out on the porch, the weather's so nice. He just won't get out. This'll be good for him.

HASKELL
    Hello, Ima.

IMA
(Going to HIM.)
    Well, back to the old stomping grounds, I guess.

HASKELL
(Taking HER hand.)
    What happened to the well?

IMA
  What? Oh, I tell you. There's been so many kids
  playing around the durn thing, I had Milton put that
  slab over the top of it. We haven't used it for years,
  anyway. Well, I thought we'd set out on the porch.
  The weather's so nice. I'll go in and roust him out.
  We're so excited y'all are here!

(SHE goes in.)

LEAH
  Those bagels . . .

HASKELL
  They're fine.

(The following exchange is muted. It is not heard by the
audience.)

LEAH
  Are you all right?

HASKELL
  Yeah, it's just—it's hard.

LEAH
  I know. Thank you.

IMA
(Pushes MILTON onto the porch in a wheelchair. HE is
completely incapacitated, wearing a hunter's cap, heavy
jacket, and slippers.)

  All right now, here we go.

150

(LEAH and HASKELL exchange glances. SHE takes HIS elbow firmly.)

Here's Leah and Haskell.

LEAH
Hello, Milton.

HASKELL
Hello, Milton, how are you?

(There is no response from MILTON.)

IMA
He's just an old crank, that's what he is.

(LEAH joins THEM at the porch, leaving HASKELL in the yard.)

Well, you know, I never realized little Milton was already graduating?

LEAH
Isn't that just amazing?

IMA
This is just the most amazing thing. Well, Dora. I guess he's off to college, or what?

LEAH
The Texas University, where else?

IMA
You're gonna have a quiet house.

LEAH
Well, but in the meantime he and his friends have started this band, and it's just awful. "The Clodhoppers."

IMA
"The Clodhoppers"?

LEAH
They play twingy-twangy songs about chickens and plowing behind a mule. You could go crazy.

HASKELL
The first Jewish hillbilly.

LEAH
So what do they know about chickens and mules?

HASKELL
He wants to be like the other boys. It's no fun just to live in town. That's not a real Texan.

(HASKELL has joined THEM at the porch.)

IMA
Well, he'd think different if he had to shovel out a stall or two before breakfast every morning.

HASKELL
Well, sure.

IMA
What a lovely day this turned out to be.

(SHE takes LEAH's hand and THEY move off alone.)

He don't look good. I just can't get him to help.

LEAH
Ima, can't he talk?

IMA
Oh, he can talk all right. But he goes up and down.
I'm scared, honey. I brought our pastor over to talk
to him. He's not really a member of the church. He
hadn't ever been baptized. Such a silly thing. You'd
think he grew up in a cave. But now it's become
. . . He just won't do it. If he dies without . . .

HASKELL
It's been a good week at the store. Very good.

IMA
Let's go see what those bagels'll do. You want to?

HASKELL
The rain is good. Farmers and ranchers. It rains,
they spend. Benefits everybody.

(IMA and LEAH go into the house. On the way, IMA shuts off the radio.)

Business is good, though. Fifteen percent up. Denim
especially, but that's the war. Oh! Mo, Morty? In
the service. Yeah! Real soldiers.

(HE removes photos from HIS wallet.)

See? Oh! Look, look, look. The Navy. First Harelik in a boat in . . . woo!

(No response from MILTON. Pause.)

You're right, what you said, Milton. I came to this town like a dog. I licked your hand. I had no dignity. My wife came and I was ashamed. Ashamed before her and ashamed before you. For Leah, she had to give up more than I could repay. But she's so strong, you know. She made me forget how much I owe her. For you, I couldn't forget. I looked at you, I was a child in debt. Not just money—everything. Everything. And there comes a time when you have to say, "No more. I've paid you back. Let me be a man!"

(HE leans very close.)

You sonofabitch. You saved my life. I wish I could save yours.

(LEAH and IMA return. HASKELL, having seen no response from MILTON, moves away.)

IMA
Well, they came out real good. So come on up and help yourselves, everybody.

LEAH
Except I busted the wax in the jelly, so look out. There's still some little pieces.

HASKELL
Leah, I think we can go now.

IMA
Oh no, now ya'll don't have to go so soon, do you?

LEAH
Haskell?

HASKELL
We had a good visit, Ima. A real good visit.

LEAH
Is anything . . . ?

HASKELL
(Shakes HIS head.)
No. Let's go.

(LEAH nods to IMA.)

IMA
Well, all right, then. We're so glad ya'll came over.

(With sudden emotion.)

I just love you.

(HASKELL leaves LEAH's side and approaches MILTON.)

HASKELL
Goodbye, Milton.

LEAH
Goodbye, Milton. You take care of yourself.

155

HASKELL
(To IMA.)
  Goodbye.

LEAH
(To IMA.)
  We'll see you soon.

IMA
  Y'all come.

(THEY leave.)

MILTON
  Goodbye.

IMA
  Haskell!

(THEY're gone. To herself.)

  He says goodbye.

Scene Eight

LEAH is in HER kitchen, preparing the Sabbath challah.

IMA
(At the front door.)
  Leah, honey, are you home?

LEAH
  Ima?

IMA
  Yes.

LEAH
  I'm in the kitchen. Come on back.

(IMA enters.)

  How's the working woman?

IMA
  Oh! How can you cook in this heat?

LEAH
  Shabbos.

IMA
  Dora! Was this Friday? Where has the week gone?
  The working woman has sore feet.

LEAH
  How did you do today?

IMA

I sold a handbag and two longline girdles. Period. I never realized they actually had to get out there and sell.

LEAH

You just take your time. Haskell is so happy to have you in the store.

IMA

I'm sure I'm only in the way down there . . .

LEAH

No.

IMA

. . . but I tell you, I was losing my mind—wandering around the house. I'd stop and stand in one place for the longest time. You know I've never really *worked* in my life. I don't think anyone but Haskell would let me get in the way like I'm doing. . . .

LEAH

You're not in the way, Ima!

IMA

Well, uh huh . . . Let me do something here, darlin'. What can I do?

LEAH

Here. This dough is about ready to punch down.

IMA

Oh good. I'll make like this is that new fella from Fort Worth that's moved into the old Embry place.

Hamilton County will
Back the Attack

(SHE gives the dough a good punch.)

He bought the bank today.

LEAH
  Ima! What? You sold the bank?

IMA

I'll tell you something I found out. Learn your husband's business. When I saw all those papers and
documents and holdings and trusts . . . It's not that
he left me in a mess. He just never expected to die.
Really. You don't know. But the main thing is I
want to be away from the bank. You look at those
rock walls and it has his face.

(Pause.)

Did we hear from little Milton today?

LEAH
(Shakes HER head.)
Morty's on a boat in the Pacific, you know. Mo,
Mr. Hotrod, still driving a tank in Africa. And my
baby? Who knows? The Air Corps. Big secret.

IMA

Couldn't you just spit? I'll swan, if I'd had the salt to
slap him sometimes, I'd a-done it. He never did
accept Jesus. I begged him. "You don't know what
you're doing. You can't die without Jesus." "No," he
said, "No. I don't need any help." He lay there all
those weeks and I could see God's hand on him. He
got thinner and thinner until his poor soul just lay
shimmering on the bed. And he was so scared. "Take
the comforting hand of Jesus. I can't go with you,
but Jesus can. Just believe." "No," he said. "For me,
then, do it for me. How can you die without Jesus?"
And all he would say was, "No. No. No." He's lost,
Leah. His blessed soul is lost.

161

(SHE breaks.)

How can God let that happen? What is heaven if my husband isn't there? My God, then I don't want it. I don't want it.

(SHE weeps bitterly.)

What do I do?

(LEAH takes IMA in HER arms. As the women hold each other, HASKELL enters the front yard. HE carries a shovel and a tall, scrawny sapling, its roots bound in burlap.)

HASKELL
(Calling inside.)
  Leah?

LEAH
  Yes, Haskell?

HASKELL
  Leah, come out here.

LEAH
  What is it?

HASKELL
  Just come out here. I need you for a minute.

LEAH
  Just a minute, Haskell. Ima's here.

HASKELL
Oh, good. I need both of you.

LEAH
Well . . .

IMA
No, no, I'll be right out. Just let me set a second.

LEAH
(Leaving the kitchen.)
What's the big rush?

HASKELL
Well, come out here and you'll see!

(IMA composes HERSELF in the kitchen. LEAH comes onto the porch.)

LEAH
So what's so important out here?

HASKELL
I got the tree.

LEAH
This little stick?

HASKEL
Don't wither it before it's in the ground. Come hold it up so I can get the dirt in.

(IMA comes onto the porch.)

163

Oh, good, Ima. I'm glad you're here.

LEAH
It's for the boys. But why all of a sudden? Did you hear something? Is something wrong?

HASKELL
Now don't start getting excited.

LEAH
Tell me!   -

HASKELL
(Takes a telegram from HIS shirt pocket.)
This telegram came to the store right after you left. Go on. Read it.

LEAH
(Reads.)
"Arrived London safe and sound. Will write soon. Love, Milton." Oh, thank you. Thank you.

HASKELL
So I thought it would be a good time.

LEAH
It's so puny. I hope it'll take.

HASKELL
All right, let's see how it looks.

(It looks pretty good.)

IMA
  Well, just look at it, would you?

HASKELL
  Yeah, not bad. It's funny, you know, we usually
  plant a tree as a kind of memory. The jujube is
  Morty. That plum tree is Mo; that plum tree is
  Milton. Newborn babies—I can hear them crying,
  me acting like a nervous case, Mr. Perry with his
  cigar.

(HE turns to the new tree.)

  But you, I want to be different. You're gonna be
  here a long time. I want you to stand up straight,
  stretch your branches to Heaven so Heaven hears.
  We gave back.

(HE holds LEAH.)

  Mama, we gave back.

*(HE recites a blessing in Hebrew, then with HIS finger-
tips, plants a kiss on an upper branch. HE looks at HIS
watch.)*

  All right, it's almost time! I'm starving to death.
  Ima, I'm glad you're here. Will you stay for Shabbos?

IMA
  If that's all right.

HASKELL
  Of course it's all right.

*(LEAH is still intent upon the tree. HE speaks quietly to
IMA.)*

  I'll go wash up. Shmuts, shmuts, shmutsik!

(HE goes in.)

LEAH
  This is for Mordechai.

(SHE plants a kiss.)

  This is for Moishe.

(Another kiss.)

  And this is for Milton.

(Another kiss.)

IMA
  For Milton.

*(SHE plants a kiss. The clear cry of a mockingbird fills the
air.)*

Epilogue

(MILTON HARELIK, the youngest son, enters in Army Air Corps dress uniform, carrying a duffel bag. He is the same actor who played HASKELL, the Russian accent replaced by Texan. The WOMEN linger at the tree.)

MILTON HARELIK

Mama's prayer did not go unanswered. I came back

Retiring . . .   Beginning . . .

HASKELL HARELIK   MILTON HARELIK
(SEE STORY ON PAGE FIVE, SECTION A)

167

from that war and so did my older brothers, safe and sound. And after they married and moved away, I stayed right here in Hamilton and watched that puny little stick they planted in 1942 grow strong and tall. In fact, that tree and I have sort of become permanent fixtures in this town.

1955. I took over the dry goods store as Papa slowed down. I say slowed down. He just shifted his activities back home. The grandkids started coming. And those

kids had children of their own. I guess he's got eleven great-grandchildren now. The last one arrived in June. A lot of little footprints around the place. Footprints and these old snapshots.

1971. I took that one. It's the last picture in our album of the two of them together. Mama passed away about five months after that, and my wife and I moved into the master bedroom—the one I was born in. (*The WOMEN move into the house and LEAH casts a last look at the tree.*)

You know, it's funny. It seems that in the last couple of years, Papa has become an immigrant once again. His mind has finally let go of the house, the store, the

family and floats freely now back to Russia. *(A distant balalaika is heard.)* Back to his boyhood home. To the cedar forests and the thatched-roof village—the green and simple times of his childhood. He speaks only Yiddish now and he claims to hear balalaikas when he wakes up. He rarely recognizes me and the kids, and Hamilton seems, well, foreign to him.

In September of '85, Papa celebrated his ninety-sixth birthday. We had a little party for him and that evening. We took him for a drive around town—and we ended up at the square. We took a turn in front of the store and I was trying to get him to recognize it. I pointed to the sign he put up there seventy-five years ago. "You see that big old sign up there, Papa? That's you. That's your *name* up there." He looked at it. "My name," he said. "My name?"

We sat there in the car for several minutes. Nobody said a word. He didn't even remember his name. He didn't remember any of it.

Not quite two years after that, he was gone.

(HE and the tree are in two pools of light. The mockingbird beckons and the lights fade to black.)